"I'm surprised at you, Katherine Hastings!"

Brad's eyes laughed down into hers. "Whatever would your Aunt Chloe think?"

"I—I don't know what you mean," Katherine stammered, her anger draining as she stared into the blue depths of his eyes. In all the years she had known him, she had never been this close to him before, had never been so aware of the sheer size and strength of him.

"I mean," he murmured huskily, "that she wouldn't have approved of your throwing yourself at a man like this."

"What?" Katherine asked, still in a daze. "I wasn't, I mean...I didn't mean to..."

"There's no need to apologize, Katie," he told her softly, teasingly, as his strong, hard arms pulled her closer and his head began lowering toward hers. "I've been wanting to do this all evening..."

Dear Reader:

Romance readers today have more choice among books than ever before. But with so many titles to choose from, deciding what to select becomes increasingly difficult.

At SECOND CHANCE AT LOVE we try to make that decision easy for you—by publishing romances of the highest quality every month. You can confidently buy any SECOND CHANCE AT LOVE romance and know it will provide you with solid romantic entertainment.

Sometimes you buy romances by authors whose work you've previously read and enjoyed—which makes a lot of sense. You're being sensible . . . and careful . . . to look for satisfaction where you've found it before.

But if you're *too* careful, you risk overlooking exceptional romances by writers whose names you don't immediately recognize. These first-time authors may be the stars of tomorrow, and you won't want to miss any of their books! At SECOND CHANCE AT LOVE, many writers who were once "new" are now the most popular contributors to the line. So trying a new writer at SECOND CHANCE AT LOVE isn't really a risk at all. Every book we publish must meet our rigorous standards—whether it's by a popular "regular" or a newcomer.

This month, and in months to come, we urge you to watch for these names—Jean Fauré, Betsy Osborne, Dana Daniels, Cinda Richards, and Jean Barrett. All are dazzling new writers, an elite few whose books are destined to become "keepers." We think you'll be delighted and excited by their first books with us!

Look, too, for romances by writers with whom you're already warmly familiar: Linda Barlow, Elissa Curry, Jan Mathews, Frances Davies, and Jasmine Craig, among many others.

Best wishes,

Ellen Edwards

Ellen Edwards, Senior Editor
SECOND CHANCE AT LOVE
The Berkley Publishing Group
200 Madison Avenue
New York, N.Y. 10016

Second Chance at Love®

FOR LOVE
OR MONEY

DANA DANIELS

A
SECOND CHANCE AT LOVE
BOOK

FOR LOVE OR MONEY

First edition published November 1984

First printing

Second Chance at Love books are published by
The Berkley Publishing Group
200 Madison Avenue, New York, NY 10016

CHAPTER ONE

As THEY MOVED in the wake of the impassive maître d'
through the quiet understated plushness of the hotel's
internationally renowned restaurant, Katherine was
pleasantly aware of eyes turning to follow the progress
she and her escort were making. Rather than vanity, it
was her own practicality that made her realize what a
striking couple they made. Even in an establishment like
this, their physical presence alone made them worthy of
a second glance.

Katherine wore white, Brad wore black. His tuxedo
was neatly tailored to fit the broad expanse of his shoulders, the narrow leanness of his waist and hips, and the
long muscular length of his legs. The darkness of his
full head of hair and mustache was a perfect match to
the color of his suit, and the pristine whiteness of his
shirt contrasted effectively with the deep bronze of his
face. Katherine knew that he was drawing every female

1

eye in the place and couldn't help being proud that she was with him.

While he was well above average in height, just over six five, Katherine didn't feel dwarfed by comparison. She was taller than most women, and with the benefit of her stylishly high-heeled sandals gave him no more than a four- or five-inch advantage. There had been times when she felt self-conscious about her height when she was with men of lesser stature, but there was no danger of that happening with Brad.

Even the dress she had chosen for the evening was a guarantee that she would not be overlooked. Its silky whiteness shimmered in the indirect light as it seductively brushed her skin while clinging faithfully to the feminine contours of her body. Its style was not one that she would ordinarily have considered, but after letting herself be coaxed into trying it on by a persistent saleslady, she had to admit that it suited her. It left one arm and shoulder bare to contrast with the stark unrelieved color of the dress, a slit on the same side of the narrow skirt giving her walking room.

But the contrast did not end with flesh against cloth. As the saleslady had so adroitly pointed out, the whole idea of the ensemble was that of contrasts. The first was that of her creamy tan skin against the color of the material. The second arose out of the fact that while one side of the dress was provocatively revealing, the other was prim by comparison. The bodice was cut at an angle from above one breast to the opposite shoulder at which a long tight sleeve was attached, closing at the wrist by a length of small covered bottons. The dress was complete in itself and required no further embellishment. The only ornamentation she wore with it was a pair of large golden hoop earrings. She felt good about her appearance and was thankful for the added self-confidence it gave her. She knew that before the evening was over she would need all the help she could get.

Arriving at a discreetly secluded table, the maître d' bowed formally and held Katherine's chair for her. Just as she had known it would be, the service was predictably efficient and quietly unobtrusive.

Brad smiled warmly across the table. "It's been years since I've been here, Katherine," he commented as he glanced around appreciatively at the subtle but luxurious furnishings and decor. "And I really don't think I've come across anything in all my travels to top it. Thank you for asking me."

"You're more than welcome, Brad." She smiled as she spoke, then grimaced slightly, her eyes falling to her hands, where her fingers played idly with the stem of her wineglass. "But try to remember that my motives aren't altogether altruistic. I did warn you that this was to be a business dinner."

"Warning duly noted and appreciated." He grinned. "But surely that doesn't mean that we can't enjoy ourselves, does it?"

"No, of course not." Katherine smiled as she lifted her gaze to meet his. For a time neither spoke as they sat watching each other across the small candlelit table, and Katherine could feel her pulse rate accelerate at the interest she saw sparkling in his eyes.

Breaking the silence but not the electric awareness passing between them, Brad said, "You know, I'm finding it hard to reconcile the sophisticated lady you are today with the little pigtailed terror you were the last time I saw you."

Katherine wrinkled her nose. "Don't exaggerate, Brad. I was seventeen years old at the time, feeling very much the young lady and eager to impress you with my new, grown-up image. I was crushed when you treated me no differently than you ever had."

"Were you really?" Brad's face crinkled with amused interest.

"Scout's honor. I moped around the house for an entire week."

"And I didn't even know." Brad sighed with exaggerated regret. "I only hope I didn't do any permanent damage to your budding feminine psyche."

"Nothing you would notice." Katherine smiled. "And anyway, I really didn't blame you. There was a gorgeous redhead hanging all over you at the time, and I knew I wasn't up to such stiff competition. I did think, though, that my newfound sophistication deserved more than a pat on the head and a casual 'How's tricks, Katie?'"

Brad's deep blue eyes glittered with amusement and his strong, melodious laugh made her smile, too. "Surely I couldn't have been so insensitive," he protested.

Katherine nodded solemnly. "Those were your exact words. They're indelibly printed in my memory under the category of my most humiliating moments."

At that moment they were interrupted as their waiter served the first course before withdrawing discreetly.

"Is it too late to apologize for my crassness, or did I go too far to expect forgiveness?" Brad asked as they started on their shrimp cocktails.

Katherine cocked her head as though considering her answer. "Well, I suppose in the interest of past friendship I'll have to forgive you, but only on the condition that you never again call me Katie. I've never let anyone get away with that."

"And now I've forfeited the privilege?"

Katherine nodded. "That'll teach you to ignore me in favor of a buxom redhead."

"Was she buxom?" Brad laughed.

"Oh, yes." Katherine scowled. "Definitely. She made me feel quite insecure. Besides, why are you asking me? Don't you remember?"

Brad shook his head. "She was just one in a string of beautiful faces and accommodating bodies. At the time I was so busy enjoying my life as a free-wheeling bachelor that none of those women stands out in my memory."

Katherine sat mesmerized as his gaze intently slid over her face and form, starting with her thick honey-blond hair which framed her face. She knew the style suited her even though she had once been told that it made her head seem too heavy to be supported by the fragility of her slender neck. Her hair was forgotten as she felt the heat of his eyes dropping to her full breasts, faithfully outlined by the clinging material of her dress. After what seemed an age he raised his head to look deeply into her eyes of pansy-brown.

"But I remember you, Katie," he murmured, his husky voice as smooth as a caress across her bare skin. "Quite well. Although, as I said, I'm having some trouble reconciling the girl of my memory with the woman you are today. And just for the record, you've outgrown your insecurity very nicely."

"My insecurity?" Katherine questioned warily, aware of the pounding of her heart and the shortness of her breath as he took inventory of her appearance.

Brad lifted an expressive brow, the corner of his mustache moving in amusement. "The redhead," he prompted.

It took a moment before Katherine realized to what he was referring, and when she did color flooded her cheeks and she had to quell the desire to wrap her arms around her bosom to shield it from his penetrating gaze. Deciding it prudent to ignore his teasing comment, particularly in view of the proposition she intended to put to him later in the evening, she abruptly changed the subject. "So what have you been doing with yourself? It's been what, seven or eight years since you went away and broke my heart? Uncle Robert never gave any details, just that you were representing Donovan's overseas."

The smile on Brad's face made it clear he had seen through her diversionary tactics, but he let it go unchallenged. "That about covers it. But I have been home for brief periods over the years. I wasn't completely exiled, but I never ran into you again, from the time you were seventeen. I wonder why?"

"I don't know. I suppose I was away at school. In any case, I don't imagine my father would have tried too hard to let me know you were in town. He never did forgive Aunt Chloe for marrying your father."

"He made that pretty obvious, didn't he? I've often wondered if it wasn't because he wanted her for himself after your mother died."

Katherine shrugged. "I wouldn't have thought so, but if that were the case, I don't blame Aunt Chloe for choosing Uncle Robert. He's a much warmer person than my father ever was. I don't think Dad ever really cared about anything but the business." Her eyes clouded momentarily as memories best left untapped flashed across the screen of her mind. Shaking off the moment of melancholy, she smiled brightly, saying, "But we were talking about you. What's next in your plans? Are you just touching home base before taking off again?"

Brad shrugged his broad shoulders. "I haven't entirely made up my mind. Traveling the world loses its glamor after a while. I've been everywhere and seen everything, and I'm seriously thinking of settling down. Dad's not getting any younger, and I think it's about time I took some of the load off his shoulders."

Katherine studied him warily through the veil of her heavy dark lashes. This was a contingency she hadn't counted on. "Oh, I hadn't realized," she stated flatly. "I just supposed that this was another visit."

"Don't sound so thrilled," Brad said dryly as he took another sip of his wine. "What's the matter, were you hoping that this meeting would last you another ten years?"

Katherine laughed but could not prevent the color from rising in her cheeks. "That's not what I meant at all, and don't exaggerate. It's only been seven or eight years, closer to eight, I guess, because I was seventeen then and I'm now twenty-five."

"So old so soon," Brad teased. "Just think how quickly the years have flown. But seriously, don't you think Dad might be better off if he slowed down a bit?"

Even though Brad's determination to relieve his father of some of his duties did not exactly fit in with her plans, Katherine had to be honest. "Now that you mention it, the last time I saw him I did think he'd lost some of his old sparkle. I didn't pay it a great deal of attention at the time, but I remember he said something about having outlived two wives, and that it was time to either slow down or take another one."

Shaking his head, Brad laughed. "That sounds just like him. But truthfully, he never did regain his zest for life after he lost your Aunt Chloe. Funny, I never thought of it before, but you look a great deal like her. Maybe that's why you've always been such a favorite of my father's; you remind him of her."

"If that's the case, I'm flattered, though I'm afraid I

don't see much resemblance myself. Other than our height. Chloe was tall, too."

Brad looked suddenly nostalgic. "Dad always said it was the first thing that attracted him. He didn't like small women. He said it put a crick in his back—bending over to hear what they were saying."

Katherine smiled. "That sounds like Uncle Robert. And whether he was serious or not, both of the women he married were tall. I never knew your mother, of course, but I always understood that she was of above-average height."

Brad nodded. "I was only a kid when she died, but I can remember the two of them together. They made an impressive couple, but then so did he and Chloe."

He studied her silently as the waiter removed the dishes from their first course and served the next. When they were again alone, he said, "And you're wrong if you think it's only your height that you inherited from your aunt. You have her coloring, her eyes, even her nose. The biggest difference is in the chin; hers was never so aggressive as yours."

"Ah, well," said Katherine, airily dismissing his summation, uncertain whether to be flattered or hurt. But upon further reflection, hurt seemed to win out. "I suppose it's only natural that I take after my father in some respect, but it wasn't very diplomatic of you to mention the fact that I have the chin of a prizefighter."

Brad smiled at her indignation, and even though Katherine was slightly irritated with him, she could not help but be fascinated by the shining blue depths of his eyes or the way his mustache twitched at one corner when he was amused. The mustache was new since the last time she'd seen him. And although as a teenager she had not thought his looks could be improved, the woman in her had to admit that the thick neatly trimmed mustache only enhanced his looks. The aura of masculinity surrounding him was an almost tangible force, and she didn't wonder that she had been so bowled over by him as she was growing up. But, she reminded herself, she was no longer an impressionable child, and she would not allow herself to be swayed by his charm.

The hint of amusement still apparent in his smile, Brad reached across the table, his long fingers gently brushing her jaw before cupping the chin in question in the palm of his hand.

And despite her resolve Katherine felt a shiver of awareness tingling up and down her spine. She felt the need to break the spell as his eyes held hers mesmerized, but she seemed to have momentarily lost the use of her tongue. Not one of the witty remarks with which she normally shielded her sensitive inner self came to mind. She could do nothing but sit staring deeply into the eyes of this man she had known most of her life but whom she really didn't know at all.

She remembered with utter clarity the moment they had met. It was at the wedding of Brad's father and her aunt. Brad had been a gawky teenager, all legs and arms, and she had been a shy, introverted five-year-old overcome with the honor of having been asked to be flower girl at her aunt's wedding. Being a favorite of her dead mother's sister, she had spent a lot of time in Brad's home during the ensuing years, but the ten-year gap in their ages had been too great to be comfortably breached. He had treated her with awkward condescension while she had been in awe of him.

Entering adolescence, she had hero-worshiped him while he hadn't known she was alive. But that, she reminded herself, was a long time ago. She was no longer the innocent, long-legged, big-eyed teenager nursing the biggest crush of the century. She was a mature woman who knew who she was and where she was going. Her reason for approaching Brad this evening had nothing to do with those long-ago, deeply buried pangs of adolescent first love.

So deep was she in thought that she was startled when Brad at last broke the silence. "There is nothing about you," he said huskily, "that even remotely resembles a prizefighter. You've grown into one lovely lady right from the top of your shining hair right down to the tips of your elegant, handmade Italian shoes."

Katherine laughed self-consciously. She might no longer be the gauche teenager of yesteryear, but she was still uncomfortable accepting personal compliments. "If size nines can be described as elegant," she said wryly. "Even if they're Italian and handmade."

Moving her head, Katherine dislodged Brad's hand from her face and she concentrated on her food for a time, trying to cover the embarrassment she felt at the intensity of his gaze, the excitement of his touch, and the seductiveness of his words. She had to pull herself together. This wasn't the way she had planned it. She wanted her proposal to be strictly business; absolutely impersonal.

It was Brad who broke the silence. "I was sorry to hear about your father, Katherine. I know it must have been hard on you even though it wasn't unexpected."

"No, Dad had been warned. After his first attack the doctors tried to tell him to slow down, but he wouldn't listen. You know how stubborn he was. Besides, Hastings Electronics was the only thing he lived for. At least he died doing what he wanted to."

"I suppose so. Still, it seems a shame. After all, he

had a daughter to think about; to live for."

Katherine laughed ruefully. "Come now, Brad! We both know I was nothing but a disappointment to him from the day I was born. No matter how hard I tried, I could never please him, because there was no way I could become the son he had wanted so badly."

The words were no sooner out of her mouth than she wished them unsaid. While she had spoken no less than the truth, she had not meant to so openly expose the vulnerability she had always felt about her father's obvious wish that she had been born male. For the most part she managed to conceal the hurt, the feeling of inadequacy hiding behind the businesslike façade she had so carefully erected years ago. She felt a certain shame at having left herself open to the perceptiveness of Brad's keen gaze.

Squirming uncomfortably in her chair, she pasted a semblance of a smile on her face, vainly searching her mind for something to say to lighten the mood. Unfortunately her usually fertile mind was suddenly as barren as a desert.

"Don't sell yourself short, Katie," Brad told her sympathetically. "If your father had wanted a son so badly, he could have married again and fathered a whole tribe of them. The fact that he didn't must mean something."

Katherine grimaced wryly. "It probably meant only that he didn't want to take the time away from Hastings to bother looking for a wife."

"Maybe, but I think you're too hard on him. Oh, I know that he wasn't the most congenial man in the world, but you have to admit that when the chips were down he must have thought pretty highly of you. He left his beloved Hastings in your hands, didn't he? What greater show of confidence could you want?"

The look on Katherine's face was a study of embarrassed chagrin. She lifted her glass and took a long swallow, the potent wine warming her insides and bolstering her flagging confidence. Setting the glass back on the table, she took a deep, steadying breath and looked directly at Brad. "From what you just said, I assume that Uncle Robert has told you nothing of the way my father structured his will?"

As the shake of Brad's head she went on. "I didn't think so." Momentarily her eyes dropped to the glass she was carelessly twirling in her fingers. "Actually that's what I wanted to discuss with you this evening."

"The business part of our dinner?"

As she nodded Brad sighed theatrically. "And here I was thinking that was just an excuse to get me all to yourself."

Katherine's travesty of a smile barely recognized his intended humor. Then pushing aside any further attempt at pleasantries, she unswervingly met the directness of his scrutiny. "I suppose the best place to start is with the will and the way Father disposed of his Hastings shares."

Brad frowned in concentration. "I didn't realize there was a problem. I just assumed he left everything to you outright. He did name you his successor, didn't he?"

"Only provisionally," Katherine said curtly, unable to disguise the disgust she felt. "Actually it's rather complicated the way the will was drawn up. Even so, my lawyers assure me that it's all perfectly legal and would be impossible to overturn." She frowned, drew a deep breath, and continued. "What it comes down to is this. The company shares were left in three lots. In the beginning I was to get forty percent. Harold—you remember him, my second cousin?" When Brad nodded, she went on. "Well, he was to get twenty percent, and the remaining forty percent was to be held in trust for one year. At the end of a year the dispersal of the shares held in trust was to be handled in one of three ways. The first option, and the one preferred by my father, was that Harold and I marry. In that event, he would have been assured that the name of Hastings was perpetuated, at least as far as the company was concerned. If that happened, I was to receive an additional ten percent of the stock and Harold was to get the remaining thirty percent, making us equal shareholders."

A frown creased Brad's brow. "And that solution doesn't appeal to you? I seem to remember hearing at one time that you and your cousin were considered quite an item."

"Yes," Katherine said uncomfortably. "Well, it was no secret. She lowered her head slightly. "We used to be engaged. At that time I saw no problem in complying with my father's wishes. However, the situation has changed and there is now no way I could possibly go through with marrying him."

For several moments Brad looked at her so intently, Katherine had the uneasy feeling that he was looking straight into the deepest recesses of her mind. At last he said, "So that leaves two options yet to be explored."

Katherine sighed in relief that he chose not to inquire too closely into her reasons for breaking her engagement with Harold. No one liked to feel they'd been made a fool of, and she could view the debacle that had ended her romantic dreams as nothing less than a disaster. "If possible," she said coldly, "the second option is even more abhorrent than the first. If I fail to marry—not necessarily Harold, but anyone—within a year following my father's death, Harold gets the entire remaining forty percent of stock, giving him a controlling sixty percent to my forty percent."

Brad shook his head in disbelief. "That was pretty drastic, wasn't it? Especially since you were trained to run the firm, and from what I've heard, you've been doing a great job even though you're awfully young to have taken on that kind of responsibility."

Katherine's mouth twisted in a smile of derision at what she considered patronizing sympathy. "Don't you want to add 'for a woman'?" She'd heard that line often enough in the past to know the routine.

Smiling, he shook his head. "Don't put words into my mouth, Katie. I assure you I don't feel the need to qualify my original statement. From everything I've heard about it, it appears you've done an outstanding job of heading Hastings regardless of your age or sex."

Stated so categorically, Katherine had to believe it was sincere and she flushed with pleasure at the compliment. "Thank you," she said simply. "I'm sorry if I sounded skeptical, but I'm afraid I have a thing about sex discrimination. It always amazes me when people think of one's accomplishments only in terms of one's sex. Sex should be important in only one aspect of life," she said heatedly.

"Oh?" he grinned. "And what aspect is that?"

"Biological reproduction, of course," was her immediate reply. "Only for that purpose should a person's sex become a consideration."

Brad threw back his head and laughed outright at her vehement intensity. "I wouldn't touch that on a bet!" he said emphatically.

Katherine thought that possibly she should have been affronted by his laughing dismissal of her words, but surprisingly she wasn't. He had such an attractive laugh, deep and big like the man himself. Unable to prevent a blush from rising in her cheeks, she apologized. "I'm sorry if I came on a bit strong, but regardless of what you think about my father's preparing me for my position, believe me, sex discrimination is a wall I've been beating my head against all of my life. I'm afraid Dad was just making the best of a bad situation, since I was his only child."

Brad shrugged. "Perhaps, but the fact remains that he did see to it that you were trained to fill his shoes. I find it hard to believe he would go to all that effort, then cut you out."

"I suppose it was his way of making sure I went ahead and married Harold," Katherine said thoughtfully. "After all, even though we're only second cousins, his last name is Hastings and that was all-important to my father."

"You can't know that for certain," Brad pointed out. "But in any case, I'm not going to argue the point with you; you knew him better than I did. And getting back to his will, you've explained the first two options but you said there were three?" He looked at her expectantly.

"Yes," Katherine said uneasily. The moment of truth was painfully near, and no matter how hard she tried to convince herself that this was no different from any other business proposition, she knew better. When his father had first suggested that she approach Brad, she had thought that the fact that she knew him, knew his family, would make it easier. But when it came to the crunch, she found that wasn't the case. It had been years since she had last seen him, and there was little similarity between the sophisticated man of the world sitting across from her and the open-faced youth she had worshiped from afar.

Clearing her throat and calling on the full force of her willpower, she went on to explain the extent of the peculiarities connected with her late father's will. "According to the third option of the will, if rather than marry Harold I marry someone else within the year, someone who meets with the approval of the board of trustees, the stock left in trust will be assigned to my husband."

"And?"

Nervously Katherine watched her lifeless fingers arranging and rearranging the silverware beside her plate as though the action were completely outside her own orbit of understanding. Hesitantly she glanced up at him through the thick screen of her lashes. "Well, I've talked it over with Uncle Robert—he's one of the trustees, you know—and, well, we thought we might look into the possibility of a merger between Hastings Electronics and Donovan's Incorporated."

Brad's raised brows expressed his surprise. "You've discussed this with my father?"

Katherine nodded. "He has no objection, if you're agreeable. In fact, it was actually his suggestion."

Brad looked dumbfounded. "I'm having trouble taking this all in," he admitted wryly. "After what you've just told me, I'm afraid I don't see the feasibility of a merger, and I'm surprised my father approved the idea. I mean, I don't see what you hope to accomplish. Any merger at this point would just sweeten the pot that much more for Harold when and if he does eventually step into your shoes. I just don't get it," he confessed in bewilderment.

Even by the indifferent light from the candle on the table between them, Katherine knew the color rising to her cheeks would be perfectly visible. "You're forgetting option three, Brad," she reminded him quietly.

"Option three? You mean whereby you marry someone other than Harold? But I still don't get it. If you're planning on marrying someone else, what's the big push for a merger now? Why not wait and . . ."

All of a sudden a deadly stillness came over both of them as they sat staring into each other's eyes like two wax figures caught for all time in that one moment's pose.

At last Brad expelled his breath, the air rushing out of him as it would from a deflating balloon. His grin was lopsided as he shook his head. "Well, well, well." He sighed. "Little Katie."

As he sat there watching her with a silly grin on his face and his deep-blue eyes dancing with amusement, Katherine felt herself going hot and cold all at once. Wave after wave of ice cold followed by searing heat coursed through her body as she watched him wordlessly, half expectantly and half in dread, waiting for his decision.

At last, when Katherine was at the point of exploding in her anxiety, Brad spoke again. "Just to make sure I have the facts straight, am I correct in thinking that you're asking me to marry you?"

Katherine opened her mouth to speak, but nothing came out. Swallowing the lump that was blocking her throat, she tried again. "Yes, Brad, I am," she managed to whisper as she continued to stare at him unblinkingly.

The fatuous grin was still in place. "Well, well, well, little Katie," he said again.

"I wish you'd stop saying that!" Katherine snapped, coming to the end of her patience. The pressure of having had to make the proposal in the first place was bad enough. Waiting for his answer was agonizing, and his irreverent treatment of the situation was more than she could take.

"Saying what?" he asked innocently.

"You know very well what! 'Well, well, well,'" she said sarcastically, "as though it were some darned litany. And I've told you before, don't call me Katie!"

There was no doubt but that Katherine's temper had begun to fray around the edges. Confronting him with her unorthodox proposal had been more of a strain than she had imagined it would be, and she had known all along that it wouldn't be easy. She had tried to be as calm and businesslike as possible in such an unusual situation, but she could take only so much, and she had lashed out at him without thinking, in the heat of the moment, without even caring what his response might be. If she had taken time to consider the consequences of her outburst, she might have feared she had blown any chance for his compliance.

In any case, she certainly would never have expected him to react the way he did. His full-bodied laugh drew stares from diners at nearby tables and Katherine wished very much that she had the nerve to stuff her napkin in his mouth.

With his laughter barely under control, he chortled gleefully, "How can you quibble about a little thing like my using your childhood nickname when you've just asked me to marry you? Surely that gives me special privileges." His eyes were brimming with mischievous amusement, his smile sparkling beneath his twitching mustache as his eyes roved over her boldly, leaving her in no doubt as to what privileges he was referring.

His suggestive appraisal drew a new flood of color which scalded its way up her neck into her face. The very fact of her embarrassment humiliated her. She was a mature, sophisticated woman of the world, and she thought she had long past outgrown the habit of blushing like a schoolgirl. Tonight had proved her wrong. "That remains to be seen," she snapped. "You have yet to accept my proposal."

His enigmatic smile told her nothing about his ultimate decision. She was becoming more and more uncomfortable under his lazy-eyed scrutiny before he finally broke the spell by saying, "First, I think it best if we make sure we've got all of our facts straight. Now, as I understand it, you're saying that forty percent of Hastings would become legally mine if we marry. Is that right?" At her nod, his brow furrowed in a frown. "I'm still not sure that I understand your reasoning. It seems that you're simply exchanging one unfair arrangement for another. Either way you're losing the forty percent of the stock left in trust. In other words, what's the advantage to you, other than rubbing Cousin Harold's nose in it? Or is that reason enough in itself?"

Katherine grimaced at his barrage of questions. "I'm not altogether vindictive, but by the same token you might suspect that neither am I entirely altruistic. I'm a businesswoman, and naturally I expect to get something out of our, er, our relationship."

A teasing grin lit his entire face, offering a mischievous aura of seduction that was hard to resist. "Oh, I'm sure that if we decide to go ahead with this, we can both count on getting something out of it," he assured her solemnly.

"In the business sense," she said sternly, setting him straight—even though she was finding it difficult not to succumb to his playfully seductive attitude. While it was true that years ago she had nurtured a king-size crush on him, she thought she had surely outgrown such foolishness long ago. When his father had suggested Brad as an answer to her problems, she had felt sure that she could handle the situation in an entirely businesslike manner, but now she was assailed by doubts. The intervening years since they had last met had only served to intensify Brad's attractiveness. And what made it even more difficult was the fact that he was no longer treating her like a little cousin to be tolerated for the sake of family. No, if that gleam in his eye was anything to go by, he saw her quite differently now.

She looked up into his eyes and found her fears confirmed. All of the remembered sexual magnetism was still there along with this new and disturbing element—his acknowledgment of her as a woman.

Forcing herself to concentrate on the matter at hand, she cleared her throat. "As I was saying, in a business sense I naturally do not intend to come away empty-handed. You'll recall that I spoke of my proposition as a merger. What I'm proposing is this: in exchange for the forty percent of Hastings stock you would receive upon our marriage, I'm asking for ten percent of Donovan's Incorporated along with your assurance that I will remain as director of Hastings."

"You're asking for ten percent in exchange for forty?"

Katherine nodded curtly. "We both know that Donovan's is the larger concern. Considering the relative worth of the two companies and the weakness of my own bargaining position, I feel that a forty–ten split is an equitable proposition."

For uncomfortable moments Brad studied her in a silence that was becoming painful. "You're hating this like hell, aren't you?" he at last asked, with almost clinical interest.

"That's understandable, surely," Katherine replied with some hauteur. "I'm not used to feeling at a disadvantage in my business dealings."

He again treated her to an intense scrutiny that had her squirming uneasily in her chair. "No," he finally said, easing her tension only slightly. "I can see that you're not. Little Katie has grown up. But in any case, this isn't strictly business, is it?"

"I prefer to consider it as such," she told him stiffly, finding that handling the personal side of the proposition was proving increasingly to be a problem. By sticking to business she was on familiar ground, and there she could hold her own.

"Well, then," Brad said with an almost formal abruptness, the smile leaving his lips even though there still remained a gleam in the depths of his dark-blue eyes. It was that gleam Katherine was thinking about when he continued. "Let's be sure that I have your proposal straight. If I agree to what amounts to a marriage of convenience, I am to receive forty percent of the stock in Hastings Electronics. In return for which, you would remain on as director of Hastings as well as receiving ten percent of the stock in Donovan's Incorporated. Is that correct?"

"Not quite," Katherine replied brusquely, knowing that her face was as red as the single rose in the crystal vase adorning their table, hating what she was being forced to do.

"No?" Brad inquired, his expressive brows once more in play.

Despite her embarrassment, Katherine looked him in the eye as she shook her head and said quietly, "No. You spoke of it as being a marriage of convenience."

Katherine hadn't dared to speculate on what his reaction would be—outrage, disgust, disbelief—but she never expected the burst of laughter that shook his entire massive frame and again drew the tolerant, amused glances of neighboring diners. "And it's not to be?" he asked between peals of laughter.

"You needn't sound so damned smug!" Katherine fumed, her eyes snapping angrily. She was embarrassed that he was drawing attention to them and was downright furious that he was treating the situation as a joke.

"Sorry," he gulped, his entire attitude giving lie to his apology.

"I'll just bet!" she muttered.

But when at last it appeared that he was making an effort to control himself, she sighed in exasperated defeat. "I suppose my father foresaw the possibility of my making use of that particular loophole," she said quietly. "For he further stipulated that if I married anyone other than Harold—and within three years had not produced an heir—my own stock would revert to Harold."

Brad whistled softly through his teeth, all trace of amusement gone. "That's what I call rough," he said. "Cutting you off with virtually nothing."

"Not to my father's way of thinking. As I've tried to explain, his main concern was always first and foremost the company. If I were not to have a child of my own, at least there would still be a Hastings in charge, a *male* Hastings," she added pointedly. "And as for my being cut off, it's true that I would no longer be involved with the company, but he was not totally without paternal concern. All of his other investments and personal property were left to me. In addition, I suppose he thought that if I married, my husband would be expected to support me."

"Which naturally he would be," Brad agreed.

"Not by me he wouldn't," Katherine asserted firmly. "I want to make that point very clear, Brad. If you agree to my proposal and we don't have a . . . if we, er, if there is no heir in the stipulated three-year period"—she finally found the more acceptable phrase—"then I will neither ask nor expect anything from you. You will retain your forty percent of Hastings as I will my ten percent of Donovan's and we can go our separate ways."

"Just like that," Brad commented ruefully.

If Katherine noticed a disgruntled sense of irony in his simple statement, she chose to ignore it. Pressing on, she said, "And I want you to know that during the time we're together, I'll make as few demands of you as possible."

Brad looked at her inquiringly, studying her through narrowed eyes. "Meaning?" he finally asked.

The question disconcerted her. She had thought her meaning obvious and preferred not to have to spell it out for him. "Meaning just that," she blustered uncomfortably. "I realize that you have your own life, your own, er, friends and interests, and naturally I wouldn't expect you to give them up on my account. Actually, when your father and I first discussed this situation, I was assuming that you would be continuing with your traveling."

"Somehow I don't think I'm flattered," Brad replied dryly as he removed a gold-plated cigarette case from an inside pocket of his jacket, opened it, and offered it to her. "Care for one?" he asked.

Impatiently Katherine shook her head. "Those things will kill you. Don't you read the papers?"

A faintly mocking smile twisted Brad's lips, and she wasn't sure whether it was in response to the important topic they had momentarily abandoned or whether it was her reference to a habit she deplored. Futilely she wished she had kept her mouth shut. It was no concern of hers if the man wanted to smoke himself into an early grave, although the thought of such an occurrence coming to pass caused an unexpected tightness in her chest. Still, all she had accomplished by getting on her soapbox was to put him on the defensive when she had hoped to have him receptive to her proposal.

When he eventually spoke, however, he showed no sign of being offended. Nodding, he grinned ruefully. "I just don't believe everything I read."

Even knowing that she should let the matter drop, Katherine stubbornly persisted. "But they have proof. Just the other day I was reading that a university study has proved it conclusively. Excessive cigarette smoking can cause lung cancer."

"The key word being *excessive*," he pointed out as he tapped the ash off the end of his cigarette.

"But how do you determine excessive?" she argued. "You might think you're being very moderate in your habits, but by the time you find out differently it could be too late."

With a roguish smile tugging at the corners of his mouth, Brad slowly, suggestively, let his gaze slide over Katherine, her face, her long, graceful neck, the fullness of her breasts so faithfully molded by the soft draping of her dress. "I never claimed to be moderate in *all* my habits," he told her pointedly. "Just smoking."

For a timeless moment their eyes locked in silent communication as unbidden thoughts concerning his habits other than smoking occurred to Katherine. No, she thought, he was a big man and would have a big man's appetites. She would be foolish to think otherwise. If he agreed to her proposal, would he expect her to satisfy those appetites? Would she object if he did, or would he awaken appetites of her own?

Realizing where her thoughts were straying, she looked up in relief as the waiter removed the last of their dishes and served them after-dinner liqueurs.

"I see that you're not opposed to drinking," Brad remarked as she took a restorative sip from her glass.

"What? Oh, no, of course not," she replied as she realized the reference he was making. "That is, as long as it's done in moderation."

"Ah, yes, moderation." Brad's eyes danced. "But how do you determine moderation? You might think you're drinking moderately, but then . . ." He quirked a brow and shrugged his shoulders.

Katherine looked at him steadily for a moment, then burst out laughing. "Did I really sound that priggish?"

"Just about," he admitted, smiling as his eyes appreciatively caressed the graceful arch of her neck as she threw her head back in laughter.

"Then I definitely owe you an apology," Katherine said, her good humor restored.

"Think nothing of it," he said carelessly. "If I can swallow your marriage-merger proposal, I certainly should be able to handle anything else you throw at me."

CHAPTER TWO

KATHERINE COULDN'T HAVE been more shocked if he had slapped her. She had finally began to relax, thinking the worst was over, and now he was acting as though she had insulted him.

"I don't understand," she said stiffly. "I thought my proposal straightforward enough, and it certainly was never intended to be an insult. After all, I did speak to your father about it and he saw nothing wrong with it."

Brad took a long swallow of his drink. "Ah, yes, we mustn't forget dear old Dad's part in all this, must we? Tell me, did you lay it out for him the way you have for me?"

"I don't think I know what you're talking about," Katherine mused uncertainly.

"The part about my sticking around just long enough to father your child before making myself scarce and taking up my solitary travels again. And another thing, did you spell out how undemanding you plan to be, provided that I'm discreet, of course? That goes without saying."

The words were not as reflective of his distaste as the way he said them, leaving Katherine in no doubt as to his feelings.

Holding herself stiffly erect, she looked at him levelly. "Brad," she said in a patient, pacifying tone of voice. "I'm trying very hard to understand your position in this, but I must admit I'm finding it a bit difficult."

"Have you finished?" he asked brusquely, ignoring her last statement and nodding at her half-finished drink. His face was frozen into a cold mask but his eyes burned with an intensity of emotion that Katherine could only wonder at.

Not waiting for her response, he rose and went to stand behind her chair, ready to pull it out for her.

Astounded at the turn matters had taken when she had been so sure of a successful conclusion to the evening, Katherine silently stood, feeling that if she didn't, he wouldn't be above tipping her out onto the floor—not in his present mood.

His hand gripping her elbow tightly, Brad guided her through the maze of tables, looking neither left nor right as they went. At the front door they waited until Brad's long, gleaming Continental was drawn up before them.

Wordlessly he opened the passenger door, saw Katherine comfortably seated, slammed the door with unnecessary force, then walked around the car and got in.

"Brad," Katherine began, feeling the strain at keeping the reasonableness in her voice as she tried to make sense out of his apparent anger.

"Forget it!" Brad ordered, shocking Katherine with

the forcefulness of his mood.

Not used to being treated so arbitrarily and not inclined to take it lying down, she stiffened her spine and turned angrily toward him. "Now, just a darn minute, you creep! Where do you think you get off . . ."

"I said forget it, Katie! We'll have this out when we get back to your place."

One look at the implacable set of his square jaw changed any plan she might have had to defy him. Settling stiffly into her seat, she stared unseeingly out into the night as Brad guided the big car through the city streets and up into the hills where her home was located.

After parking his car in front of her house, Brad got out and went around to open the door for her. Silently he assisted her out of the car, took possession of her arm, and headed for the front door. Stopping under the outside light, he extended his palm. "The key," he said shortly.

Katherine groped in her purse for her keys. "Now, look here, Brad Donovan," she fumed, "I don't need you or anyone else to unlock my door for me. I've been doing it for years. Even a woman can learn something that basic if she repeats the process often enough," she added scathingly.

In the dim light it was hard to say for certain, but it appeared that the frown on his face lightened, at least for the moment. In any event, he stood back and with a bowing sweep of his hands, gave her access to the door.

In her agitation Katherine fumbled with the key for a second or two before getting the door open. Stepping in, she switched on the inside light and frowned up at Brad as she watched him follow her, ready to let him have it with both barrels if he said so much as a word about her ineptness. Having her guns primed, she was a bit disappointed when he did no more than arch his brow as he walked past her into the hall and stepped down the two steps into her sunken living room.

Katherine followed him in, throwing her purse and wrap on the divan as she went. Turning to face him, her hands on her hips, she said, "All right, Mr. Macho, suppose you tell me just what the hell this is all about."

"You have no idea?"

"Not an inkling. As far as I was concerned, we were sitting there enjoying a delightful meal and discussing a business proposition when all of a sudden you started coming on like King Kong."

"A business proposition! Is that all it is to you?"

Katherine could not sustain the strain of meeting his gaze. "I realize that my proposal was perhaps a little irregular—"

Brad snorted derisively. "To say the least," he interrupted.

"Okay, so it was a lot irregular. Still, it was straightforward enough, I think, and if you would just look on it as a business proposition..."

"Just what kind of business do you think I'm in, lady?"

Katherine looked at him in confusion. "I don't understand. If you simply think of it from a business standpoint..."

"But I don't happen to be in the Stud-A-Go-Go business," Brad interjected angrily.

Katherine's face flushed brightly. "That's a rotten thing to say!" she exclaimed in shocked outrage.

"But rather to the point, don't you think? When we cut through all the inessentials, what it boils down to is that you're propositioning me. You want me to take you to bed and impregnate you. Now, isn't that the bottom line?"

"I asked you to marry me!" Katherine stormed, too incensed to even wonder how things had disintegrated to such a point.

"Oh, sure, you're willing to sign a piece of paper, and I sure as hell can't complain about the fee you're prepared to pay, forty percent of Hastings. I suppose I should be flattered. After all, I would probably be the best paid stud on the entire West Coast!"

"Stop using that word!" Katherine all but screamed at him.

"What word's that? *Stud*? What's the matter, a little too crude? But so appropriate."

All of a sudden he seemed to make an effort to control himself. Running his fingers through his hair as he restlessly paced the floor, he at last stood still, his hand massaging the tightness at the back of his neck, arching his back in an apparent effort to relieve the tension. "All right, I apologize. Maybe I'm making too much out of this, but it just seems to me that you're not looking at things realistically. You keep saying it's only business, yet you're suggesting that we live together as man and wife, the whole purpose being that we have a child together. Now, that can be done in one of two ways. There's artificial insemination and then there's the old-fashioned tried and true method of..."

"Please!" Katherine objected hotly. "I do know where babies come from and I see no need to go into it further."

"Just as you like," Brad said docilely, a rueful grin lightening his face. "But just in case you're interested, I much prefer the second method. In fact, I'd insist on it."

Katherine glared at him resentfully. "You seem to

take a perverse pleasure in trying to embarrass me, and I do wish you'd stop it. I realize that my proposal was unexpected and unusual, but there's certainly nothing sordid about it."

Loosening his tie, Brad flopped down on the divan, leaving Katherine standing to glare down at him. "You think not?" he asked as he removed his cigarette case from an inside pocket. Not waiting for an answer, he eyed her through narrowed lids as he put a cigarette in his mouth and lit it. "You're not making me feel guilty about this one," he said. "I've just discovered that circumstances count for quite a lot when determining excess and moderation, and in these circumstances I doubt that an entire carton would be considered excessive."

Katherine said nothing because she was inclined to agree with him. If he had offered her one at that point, she would have been sorely tempted to take it. Never in her wildest dreams had she envisioned that the evening would turn into such a complete fiasco. It had all seemed so simple when she had discussed the affair with Brad's father. Having to propose to any man naturally had to be looked upon as an unnerving experience, but that was what had made the idea of approaching Brad, rather than a complete stranger, so attractive. He was almost family, or so she had let his father convince her. She suppressed a tiny, niggling thought that her past infatuation with him might have anything to do with her heeding his father's suggestion.

Brad took a deep drag and expelled the smoke slowly. He sighed deeply. "Okay, you keep saying you want to look at the situation as though it were merely a business proposal. Well, if this is the way you conduct business, I can't say I'm terribly impressed."

"What do you mean?" Katherine demanded indignantly, feeling that her business acumen was beyond reproach. "You said yourself that you thought I'd done a good job of heading Hastings. Was that all a lot of hot air?"

"Of course not," he said dismissively, ignoring her anger. "From what little I know I'd say you've done an excellent job with Hastings, but in this instance you seem to be totally unprepared."

"Unprepared? What's that supposed to mean? How does a woman prepare to ask a man to marry her? Should I have sent flowers and candy? Perhaps a diamond? At least I did invite you to a candlelit, champagne supper. I'm sorry if I failed to create the right atmosphere!"

She was fuming, and it didn't help one bit to see him sitting so calmly, watching her from beneath half-lowered lids, gazing intently through the haze of smoke from his cigarette. The heat of her anger went all the way through her; her high cheekbones were bathed in the flush of her indignation. Her eyes snapped; her bosom heaved with the force of her anger. Her slim hands trembled and she lowered them to her sides.

Brad shrugged carelessly. "I wasn't referring to that type of preparation," he informed her, then grinned mischievously. "Although now that you mention it, I am partial to turtles."

Katherine's eyes widened, in disbelief. What a strange man the hero of her adolescence had become! "Turtles? You wanted turtles? Is that some kind of weird custom you've picked up in your travels? Because if it is, you can forget it! No way am I going to go all over town hunting up a turtle for you. I'll die an old maid first!"

Brad threw back his head and roared with laughter while Katherine stood looking at him in disbelief. "Stop it, you idiot!" she shouted, angry and confused.

Wiping the tears from his eyes, Brad finally got himself under control. "I'm sorry, Katie, it's just the idea of you running around in your elegant dress, your stiletto heels, peeking under bushes and rolling over rocks looking for a turtle!" Once more the laughter bubbled up in his throat and his large frame shook with the force of his amusement.

At first Katherine stood looking at him as though he were some strange species she had never seen before and didn't care if she never saw again. Then slowly the anger drained out of her and her sense of the ridiculous came through as she considered the picture he had painted. Then her own laughter bubbled forth, easy and without restraint.

As she sank down on the sofa beside him, it diminished to an occasional gurgle. "All right," she said, still smiling. "Obviously I've made a fool of myself. I accept that, but only on the condition that you explain what the devil you're talking about."

"*Candy* turtles," Brad explained gleefully. "Surely you've had them, those gooey, sticky things, caramel and chocolate-covered nuts—delicious! They're my favorite. Since you mentioned giving me candy, I thought I'd let you know for future reference. I like flowers, too, in case you're interested, red roses by preference, but I don't know about the diamond. Don't you think that's a little much? Particularly on our first date. I mean, a man has to draw the line somewhere, and I don't want you getting the wrong idea. I'm just not that kind of guy!"

Color bloomed in Katherine's cheeks and her smile was becoming strained. "All right, you've had your fun, but enough is enough. Evidently I misunderstood something you said, so suppose we backtrack and you explain just what the hell you were talking about!"

"Don't swear, darling." His casual endearment shocked her somewhat. "It's so unfeminine."

Katherine bristled. "Don't look now, darling," she drawled insinuatingly, "but your chauvinism is showing."

Smiling, he acknowledged her scored point but refused to continue the exchange. "Getting back to the subject under discussion, namely your marriage proposal, when I said you didn't seem very well prepared, I was referring to the entire premise of your proposal: that I get you pregnant. In light of that, it seems to me that you're taking an undue risk. After all, for all you know, I may be sterile. Wouldn't it have been better if you had waited until I could have taken a fertility test? Or were you planning to do that next?"

"I wish you wouldn't talk that way," she complained irritably. "You make it all seem so, so..."

"Cheap, cold-blooded, sordid?" he supplied helpfully, an eyebrow raised.

"Yes!" she exploded angrily. "That's exactly the way you make it seem, and it wasn't meant to be that way at all!"

"No? Then suppose you explain the way it was supposed to be. If I've misjudged you, then I'm sorry, but somehow the idea of a marriage proposal followed immediately by the offer that I would be allowed to fool around strikes me as something less than... flattering."

Katherine was momentarily at a loss for words. Looking at it that way, she supposed it did sound a bit unsavory.

Before she could collect herself to make a rebuttal or explain herself, Brad was speaking again. "Just by way of clarification, did you expect me to grant you the same license?"

A frown creased Katherine's brow. "I don't understand. What..."

"I mean, would you expect me to turn a blind eye if you decided to take a lover?" he demanded curtly.

"What? Why, how dare you!" Katherine fumed incoherently, totally stunned by the implication of his words.

"Don't talk to me about daring, lady." Brad had cut her off without a hint of apology. "In a one-on-one contest you'd win hands down, when it comes to raw nerve. As for my question, I think it deserves an answer. If I decide to accept your proposal, is there a chance that I'll need to shake the sheets of my bed to make sure you're not playing house on the side?"

"Don't be ridiculous!" Katherine exclaimed, her face flaming from anger and embarrassment, her pulse racing as never before.

"You don't plan on taking a lover?"

"Of course not! If I had access to this mythical lover, why in the hell do you think I would have put myself through the nightmare of proposing to you?" She had totally lost control of the situation, was beyond worrying about the fact that she was exposing her rawest emotions to the large, enigmatic man sitting beside her studying her so intently.

A grin creased Brad's face. "Since he's mythical, darling, you'll still need my services," he pointed out with prosaic logic. "And I do wish you'd quit swearing. If we marry, maybe we can work out a compromise. You quit swearing, and I'll quit smoking. Deal?"

"I'll swear if I damn well please!" Katherine all but shouted. Unable to contain her anger, she stood up, intending to demand that he leave immediately. But when she spun around, throwing her arm out to show him the way to the door, one of her heels caught and she felt herself falling. But before she could hit the floor, strong hands caught her, and in the blink of an eye she found herself sitting with the softness of her backside pressing into the hard muscular thighs of the man whose face loomed only inches above her own. She stared at him, shocked.

"I'm surprised at you, Katherine Hastings!" Brad's eyes laughed down into hers. "Whatever would your Aunt Chloe think?"

"I—I don't know what you mean," Katherine stammered, her anger draining as she stared into the blue depths of his eyes. In all the years she had known him, she had never been this close to him before, had never been so aware of the sheer size and strength of him. She continued to stare unblinking into his eyes, as though expecting to find the secrets of the universe revealed there.

"I mean," he murmured huskily, seeming suddenly to be as caught up in the spell as she was, "that she wouldn't have approved of your throwing yourself at a man like this."

"What?" Katherine asked, still in a daze. "I wasn't, I mean, I caught my heel. I didn't mean to..."

"There's no need to apologize, Katie," he told her softly, teasingly, as his strong, hard arms pulled her closer and his head began lowering toward hers. "I've been wanting to do this all evening."

Somewhere in the deep recesses of her subconscious Katherine felt she should be protesting, and opened her mouth to obey the impulse, but she never uttered a sound.

With a mastery she couldn't even have dreamed of, his mouth took hers in a kiss that made so much nonsense of any other kiss she had ever experienced. As his tongue fought a sensual duel with her own, his arms tightened around her, and after a brief moment of shock Katherine felt her body softening, becoming pliant as he molded her to his own hard contours. Seemingly with a will of their own, her arms slid up his chest to encircle his neck, her fingers burying themselves in the thick richness of his hair.

With rational thought beyond her, she gave herself up to the sensation of drowning in the sensuality of the moment. When his lips left hers to explore the creamy silkiness of her face, she automatically rested her head on his shoulder, giving him ready access to the slender length of her neck and the racing pulse at its base. At the same time, her hands were bent on an exploration of their own, compulsively measuring the width of his shoulders, the strength of his back, the satisfying angles of his face.

Without quite realizing how it happened, Katherine vaguely became aware of the fact that they were stretched out together on the couch as she felt the supple suede upholstery beneath her. If it had been her intention to protest the intensifying intimacy of their embrace, her opportunity was lost as she felt his weight pressing down upon her, his hard male body imprinting her soft, yielding flesh.

As his mouth once more covered hers, his tongue plundering the sweetness within, she lost all hold of reality, surrendering mindlessly to the multitude of sensations he was creating. Never before had such fire raced through her veins. Never before had the reasoning power of her mind so readily abdicated to the passion of her body. Never before had she given herself up so willingly to the expertise of any man's sensuality.

"Oh, sweetheart, you're so delicious," Brad moaned softly in her ear as he tasted the length of her neck with the tip of his tongue. His hand slid over the curve of her hip, his fingertips gently kneading the softness they found. As though reluctant to relinquish its newfound treasure, his hand moved upward, forging a fiery trail of discovery, pausing at her waist to gently caress, sliding possessively over her ribs, stopping to experience the wonder of her pounding heart before finding its way to the fullness of her breasts. As long fingers learned the shape and bounty of their prize, a moan of pure ecstasy escaped from deep in Katherine's throat.

Cupping the soft weight of her breast in his hand, Brad groaned into her ear. "Since the moment you opened the door to me tonight, I've wanted you." Gently his fingers traced her soft fullness, brushing lightly over hardened peaks before again cradling the exquisite softness in his palm. "No matter how businesslike you tried to be, how hard you try to deny your femininity, your lovely full breasts give you away. All evening while you were sitting across from me, telling me that ours was a business date, I've wondered what it would be like to make love to you, to taste your sweetness."

Shock and pleasure surged together through both Katherine's mind and body, his confession exhilarating to her feminine pride. And yet, somewhere in the depths of her subconscious, she couldn't help being staggered by such plain speaking. "Brad," she protested huskily, "you shouldn't talk like that."

Laughing at her disapproval, he leaned over her, propping himself up on one elbow. Running a teasing finger down her nose, he smiled. "Little puritan. What a fascinatingly contradictory female you are. Ms. Hastings, the efficient businesswoman; Katie, warm and passionate; and Katherine, soft and vulnerable and just a bit of a prude."

Katherine stared at him, wordless. "I've told you that I don't like to be called by that foolishly childish nickname," she managed, at last. It was impossible to summon up the anger and indignation she felt would be appropriate when every nerve ending was pulsating with a life of its own.

"Did you?" he asked softly as he stared down into her passion-glazed eyes. "I must have forgotten."

"Very conveniently," she said, trying to express proper indignation, but once again his mouth found hers and reawakening sensuality swamped all rational thought. Once again she was drawn into the vortex of his virile magnetism. Drugged by the eroticism of his large masculine body weighing her down into the softness of the sofa, mesmerized by the sweetness of his kisses, the gentle possessiveness of his caress, Katherine yielded completely to Brad's own special brand of charm.

Even as his hand glided down her body, entered the slit in the side of her skirt, moving arbitrarily up the smoothess of her thigh, she made no attempt to stop him but, rather, clung all the tighter to him, her lips exploring the rugged planes of his face.

"One thing's for sure, sweetheart," Brad breathed raggedly, "if I do take you up on your proposal, there's no fear that we'll find we're incompatible. You make me burn for you!"

Through the mist of passion shrouding Katherine's senses, a warning bell sounded somewhere in the deep recesses of her mind. Fevered exploration of lips and hands ceased. She lay still beneath him.

Sensing her mental as well as physical withdrawal, Brad lifted himself up on an elbow and looked down into her face. She felt as though a mask had slipped into place there. Only the heightened warmth of her cheeks and the swollen vulnerability of her lips hinted at the twisting, fevered, passion-filled woman she had been only moments before.

A look of concern on his face, Brad asked softly, "What is it, sweetheart? Did I hurt you?"

It was all Katherine could do to prevent herself from laughing hysterically. How could he be so insensitive? She had been ready to surrender herself totally into his keeping, all thoughts of wills and business arrangements banished from her mind, but to him it had been little more than a game, a testing of the water, so to speak.

She wanted to scream and curse at him. Had he hurt her? Oh, God, if only he knew!

"Would you let me up please?" she managed coolly.

As he drew away from her, a look of puzzlement on his face, Katherine sat up and straightened her clothes. Fighting to slide back behind her protective façade, she smiled stiffly. "Well, that's that, then."

Brad looked at her as though she were speaking a foreign language. "What's what?" he asked in bewilderment.

He ran his hand smoothingly through his thick hair and Katherine blanched as she remembered that it had been her feverishly impassioned fingers that had caused its disarray.

Forcing herself to concentrate on what was being said, she turned her gaze from his disturbing presence. "The end of the experiment, of course," she said in reply to his question.

Brad shook his head. "Frankly, sweetheart, you've lost me. I don't know what the hell you're talking about."

"Oh, come now," she scoffed. "There's no need to pretend. I don't blame you. After all, if you accept my proposal, our relationship will necessarily involve a close physical interaction, and I suppose it's quite natural that you would want to determine whether or not we're compatible."

The light in his eyes hardened. "And that's what you think I was doing? Making sure we're compatible?"

Katherine laughed mockingly. "Surely you're not upset with me for realizing what you were up to? I'll admit that you've got a great technique, but I can't think you actually expected me to see all this as anything more than what it was. An experiment."

As his expression changed, she regarded him with innocent disbelief. He actually seemed angry, more than angry—furious! Well, she didn't care. Her pride had been lacerated enough just by the act of proposing to him. She wasn't going to allow him to grind it into the dust by letting him guess how devastating she had found his lovemaking.

Brad shook his head, a smile of derision on his lips. "You're a real cool lady, aren't you?" he said.

"I try to be," she agreed regally, her head held high.

"But I don't think you always succeed," he mocked.

"Oh, how's that?" she asked warily. She had wanted to dispel any impression that she was in any way overwhelmed by him, to prove that she could be just as casual about their sizzling romantic interlude as he could, but she was not entirely confident of her ability to handle his unexpected attack.

"I mean that your response a few minutes ago was anything but cool. Red hot would be a more apt description."

Try as she might, Katherine could not prevent the color from rising in her cheeks, but her voice was steady as she replied, "As I said, you have a very practiced technique, but enough is enough."

Hoping to indicate that it was time he should leave, Katherine stood, and when Brad did the same she thought he was taking the hint. But he surprised her by reaching out and taking her by the shoulders. When he started to pull her close, however, she refused to submit. Angrily she twisted away from him. "Oh, no, you don't!" she told him furiously. "You've already conducted your experiment. There will be no more free samples tonight!"

"Like hell!" he exclaimed as he grabbed her wrist in a punishing grip. He gave a tug and she landed with a thud against the hard wall of his chest. Her fall nearly knocked the breath from her. Giving her no time to protest, hardly time to breathe, Brad fastened his mouth on hers in a hard, searing kiss. Gone was any pretense of teasing affection. Neither was there any question that uncontrollable passion was the driving force behind his assault. He was intent only on punishing her impertinence, and he made a thorough job of it.

When at last he pushed her from him, Katherine felt battered and bruised as she struggled to regain her breath and her composure.

"Since you're not giving out any more free samples, you can chalk that up to my account," he told her curtly. "You'll be hearing from me."

He was turning to go when Katherine's temper broke with a vengeance. Grabbing his arm with unexpected strength, she jerked him around. "Oh, no, you don't!" she shouted. "You can just forget about what I said earlier. I wouldn't marry you now if you were the last man on earth, you overgrown bully!"

A smile twitching on his mouth, Brad stood looking down at her as though amused by her disheveled appearance, her heightened color, her breasts that rapidly rose and fell with her anger. "If that were the case," he said sardonically, "you wouldn't get the chance," He reached out and carelessly ran a finger down the slender length of her nose. "You'd have to stand in line like everybody else."

"Why you—" she began furiously.

"Ah-ah," he interrupted, placing a finger over her mouth. "Don't say it, Katie. And don't look now, but your cool is slipping."

For a moment Katherine could only stand glaring up at him, but she then stepped back, took a deep, steadying breath, and pulled herself to her full height, pointlessly wishing she still had the advantage of the four-inch heels that had somehow slipped off during the heated course of the evening. Though her color was still high, she had pulled in the rein on her temper. "You're right, of course," she said calmly. "There's nothing to be gained by a slinging match. We're two intelligent adults and I'm sure you'll understand that I've decided to withdraw my proposal. I made a mistake. Although we have been acquainted for years, we really didn't know each other well enough to make the type of commitment necessary. The positive side of the situation is that we found out in time, and there's no harm done."

She stood with a show of serenity she was far from feeling, waiting for his acceptance of her summation. At this point she wasn't concerned about fulfilling the terms of her father's will; she knew only that she wanted to see the back of Brad Donovan once and for all.

Slowly he shook his head. "You give me too much credit for understanding, Katie," he told her with mocking regret. "Because I'm afraid I can't accept that. You made me an offer and I've told you I'll let you know. As far as I'm concerned, nothing has happened to change that."

"You can't mean that!" Katherine exclaimed in astonishment. "I told you I've changed my mind. I don't want to marry you. You can't make me!"

"Of course not," he readily agreed. "But there is such a thing as breach of promise. True, it's not tested very often these days, but it does still exist. Can't you just imagine the field day the newspapers would have with a story like that?"

Katherine looked at him in shocked dismay. "You— you wouldn't!" she stammered.

"Don't bet on it," he told her audaciously.

"But why?" she asked in bewilderment. "It's not as though you want to marry me, not really!"

"That's not been determined. I have yet to make up my mind."

She was outraged by the arrogance of his presumption. "You egotistical creep!" she said heatedly, any resolve to stay calm flying out the window. "If you think I'm going to sit idly by until you get around to making up your mind, you've got another think coming! You're not the only man in town who wouldn't mind owning forty percent of Hastings Electronics."

"No, but I'm the one you asked, and I have first refusal. You'll be hearing from me."

He turned and walked toward the door. With his hand on the knob he looked back at her from over his shoulder. "And Katie," he advised her grimly, "don't do anything you might regret."

CHAPTER THREE

"Don't do anything you might regret." Those words ran in circles around and around in Katherine's mind all weekend. She had already done something she regretted, and that something was proposing to Brad Donovan in the first place.

He was undeniably attractive, he was an experienced businessman, and he was family, or nearly so. She had once idolized him. When her uncle had suggested that asking his son to marry her would solve all her problems, she had let herself be persuaded. It had seemed so simple. How was she to know that he had grown into an arrogant, egotistical boor?

But that's exactly what had happened. For the first part of their evening together she had thought she had recognized the boy he had been. His teasing good nature had brought back pleasant memories, but his true colors had soon shown through, first in his indignation over her perfectly straightforward proposal, then in his angry response when she'd seen through his scheme for determining their compatibility.

She'd been angry when she said she no longer wanted to marry him, but upon reflection, with the heat of anger no longer clouding her judgment, she realized she had meant it. She was used to being the one in charge, and she didn't want to be ruthlessly overridden by anyone. As she surely would be if she gave Brad Donovan any say in her life. In addition, and possibly more important, she knew it would potentially be emotional suicide to enter into an open marriage with a man who could make her go up in flames of desire. Because no matter how mad he had made her, she couldn't deny, at least not to herself, that that had been exactly the effect he had had on her. That had never happened to her before and she was afraid a steady diet of that sort of thing could make her feel very possessive of the man who made her feel that way.

She spent a lazy day Sunday, attending late mass, picking up Chinese food for her noon meal. After she had eaten she changed into an emerald-colored bikini and spread herself out on a chaise lounge beside the pool. Her intention had been to concentrate on the dilemma in which she found herself regarding compliance with the terms of her father's will, but a full stomach combined with the warmth of the sun shining down on her was having a soporific effect.

She didn't know how long she'd been lying there, suspended somewhere between awareness and sleep, when the creaking of the gate in the fence surrounding the pool caught her attention. Through sleep-heavy eyes she looked up to see the silhouette of a tall man walking toward her. The sun was in her eyes, but the shape was alarmingly familiar and her pulse increased rapidly, only to slow and steady as the man drew nearer. Though their build was very nearly the same, this man was an older, more refined version of the man who had been almost constantly on Katherine's mind the last several days.

Sitting up, she smiled and held out her hand. "Uncle Robert, how nice to see you. I'm afraid you caught me being extremely lazy."

The tall gray-haired man squeezed her hand and leaned over to kiss her cheek. "That's what Sunday afternoons are for, aren't they?"

"Sit down and let me get you something to drink," said Katherine warmly. "What would you like?"

"Don't bother," her uncle protested, but she ignored him.

"No bother," she assured him. "Alcoholic or non?" She picked up the sheer cover-up matching her swimsuit and slipped her arms into it.

"Non," Robert told her, smiling.

She was back in a very few minutes carrying a tray holding glasses and a pitcher of lemonade. "Here we go." She filled the glasses and handed one to her uncle, then reappropriated her seat on the lounge.

"Lovely day," she said uneasily. Usually there was no one she was happier to see than her uncle by marriage, but today she was still feeling particularly vulnerable. What a disaster had ensued from his suggestion that she ask his son to marry her, as a means of solving her business problems! Not that she blamed Robert; it was just that she would rather not have to recap for anyone what had transpired last Friday night.

"But then it's rarely anything but, is it?" he said, confusing her by breaking into her dark thoughts.

"What?" she asked, thinking that she must have missed something.

"A lovely day," he said by way of explanation. "Here in sunny California we seldom have anything else, do we?"

"Oh, no, I guess that's true. No wonder people flock here in droves."

Silence followed that brilliant bit of deduction as she and Uncle Robert sat quietly staring off into space. At last Katherine could stand it no longer. "It didn't work out, you know!" she blurted out, surprising herself. She hadn't meant to discuss it.

Indicating that he knew exactly what she was talking about, Robert regarded her gravely. "What went wrong?" he asked.

Katherine shrugged. "I don't really know."

"Did you ever get around to proposing?"

"Oh, yes." Katherine laughed mirthlessly. "I managed to make just about as big a fool of myself as it's possible to do."

"What makes you say that?"

Katherine looked at him, a frown creasing her brow. "Look, Uncle Robert, can't we forget it? Okay? Let's just say I blew it and leave it at that."

Robert shrugged carelessly and silence once more descended, only to be shattered when Katherine broke her own ban on the subject of her aborted proposal. "Your son has got to be the most arrogant, egotistical, bad-tempered bully I have ever had the misfortune to meet!"

Robert seemed surprised at her vehemence. "Brad?" he exclaimed.

"Do you have more than one son?" Katherine snapped.

Trying unsuccessfully to suppress a smile at his niece's uncharacteristic display of ill humor, he regarded her for a long moment. "Not to my knowledge. So I'll have to assume you're talking about Brad. But what did he do to give you such a poor opinion of him?"

"I said I didn't want to talk about it," Katherine reminded him firmly, completely ignoring the fact that she was the one who introduced the subject.

Another period of silence followed. "He practically accused me of being immoral!" she said, breaking her own stricture.

Robert waited patiently, seemingly not willing to risk being reprimanded a second time.

"He also said I was a prude!"

"That appears to be a contradiction in terms," Robert pointed out quietly. "How can you be immoral and a prude at the same time?"

"Damned if I know," Katherine retorted. "And that's another thing, he says I swear too much." She was silent for a moment, then added, "Of course, that was after I got on his case for smoking so much. He said if we married, we'd have to compromise. He'd give up smoking if I gave up swearing."

Robert's brows rose in a gesture reminiscent of his son. "Oh?" he said speculatively. "Then he didn't refuse outright?"

"What? Oh, no, not right away. At first I thought he was going to agree, then all of a sudden he was right off the wall, mad as hell. He practically dragged me from the restaurant!" she said, remembering the scene with a new flood of indignation.

"I see," Robert remarked contemplatively. "Did something happen between the time that you thought he was receptive to your proposal and when he became angry?"

Katherine shrugged petulantly. "Nothing that I can think of. He had asked for a clarification of my proposal. I tried to be completely fair, explaining the terms of

Father's will and making it plain that I would try not to let our arrangement interfere with his life any more than was absolutely necessary."

"A-a-a-h, I see," Robert murmured knowingly, a smile tugging at the corner of his mouth. "And that was when he jumped up and dragged you out of the restaurant?"

Katherine nodded curtly. "I was never so embarrassed in my life. There were any number of people there that I knew."

"Yes, well, I can see how that would upset you," her uncle said sympathetically. "So what happened next?"

She took a moment to reflect on what was being asked, then decided that she could not discuss with her uncle what had happened after she and Brad had arrived home. "I'd really prefer not to discuss it," she said. "If you want a blow-by-blow account, you'll have to talk to Brad. No doubt he'd be only too happy to tell you in vivid detail how I let him make a fool of me!"

"Oh? I thought you said you had made a fool out of yourself."

"That was earlier. Later he was only too happy to help."

"And how did he do that?"

"Never mind." She grimaced. "Suffice it to say that it was an idea that didn't work out."

"Then he flatly refused?"

"No, he said he'd think about it."

"And?"

"I told him to take a hike. If he thinks I'm going to sit on my thumbs waiting until he condescends to give me an answer, he can think again. He's not the only man in the world."

"Of course he's not," Robert staunchly agreed.

Silence followed only to be broken when Robert inquired quietly, "Do you have anyone else in mind?"

Katherine's shoulders slumped. "No," she admitted forlornly.

"Is there any chance that you and Harold Hastings might make it up?"

"No!" she said emphatically. "That I do know. Nothing will ever induce me to marry that two-timing—er, creep." She quickly modified her choice of words. Maybe Brad was right. Maybe she did swear too much. "Anyway, marrying Harold is no longer even an option as far as I'm concerned. I never did tell you what happened. Actually I've never told anyone. I don't want to think about it, to remember the humiliation, but you can take my word for it that what I found that day you asked me to stop by his apartment and pick up that Martin file was enough to put me off him for life. We were supposed to be engaged, for godsake!"

The look on the dignified gentleman's face was a study in innocence. "So where does that leave us?"

"I don't know," Katherine admitted, her spirits sagging. She had considered the problem off and on all weekend and was no closer to a solution now than when she had started.

"Charles has been dead how long now? Eleven months?"

Katherine nodded. She knew the time factor was becoming critical, and she fought down the urge to panic. According to her father's will she had one year—twelve short months—to make an acceptable marriage and retain her interest in Hastings. Eleven months had gone; only one was left. She had no idea what she was going to do.

At the sound of the gate opening both she and her uncle turned to see who was there, and the sight of the familiar, large-framed man making his way toward them caused Katherine's heart to jump to her throat. There was no mistake this time who it was.

Brad barely nodded in her direction before turning to his father. "Dad, I didn't expect to find you here," he said dryly.

"Oh, yes," his father said expansively as he reached over and squeezed Katherine's hand. "Katherine and I usually manage to get together at least once during the weekend." He got out of his chair and sat down beside Katherine on the lounge, not letting go of her hand. "Here, son, you can sit there," he said amicably, nodding toward his recently vacated chair. "We've become very close over the years, haven't we, my dear?" he said to Katherine.

Not waiting for her answer, Brad's mouth twisted into a sneer. "How cozy."

"Yes, isn't it?" Robert agreed cheerfully as he put an arm around Katherine's shoulders and gave her a hug. "I've become very fond of this girl, I can tell you," he reiterated, planting a fond kiss on her cheek.

Katherine squirmed uncomfortably before the blast of icy disdain directed at her from Brad's eyes. She didn't know what her uncle thought he was up to, but she certainly wasn't used to this . . . this display of his affection. She was very fond of him and knew the feeling was reciprocated, but they had never been overly demonstrative with each other. The fact that he had chosen this moment to change their relationship both dismayed and embarrassed her. Brad sat watching them, a look of blatant disapproval on his face.

Eager for any excuse to break the almost tangible tension, Katherine jumped to her feet. "If you'll excuse me, I'll get you a glass and you can join us for lemonade."

She knew she sounded like the parody of a not too bright schoolgirl and was furious at herself for it. But she could think of nothing else to say.

That Brad agreed with her was all too evident. "Lemonade, for godsake!" he said scornfully.

Katherine's backbone stiffened as she stood glaring down at him. "If you don't want lemonade, then what would you like?" she asked ungraciously.

"Whiskey, a double," Brad ordered brusquely.

"Shall I pour it into a glass or would you rather slug it straight from the bottle?" Katherine asked with icy sweetness. She didn't need this. She hadn't invited him here, had no idea why he was here, and she wasn't about to put up with his sarcastic disapproval.

Robert jumped to his feet. "Why don't you let me get it, honey? I know where everything is." Without waiting for her assent, he turned and walked toward the house.

Katherine watched his disappearing back with regret. She had hoped to escape long enough to make a quick change of clothes and run a comb through her hair. She knew she looked a mess, her hair falling haphazardly from a knot on top of her head, her long bare limbs gleaming with suntan oil, the light cover-up she wore actually covering very little.

Looking at Brad, she felt at a terrible disadvantage. He looked very good himself. He was dressed casually in bluejeans and a white knit pullover, both serving only to emphasize his rugged handsomeness as they pulled tautly over muscles that were blatantly male. The bright sunlight put a gloss on his thick black hair, his gleaming sunkissed skin clearly no stranger to the power of nature. Even though she was angry with him, she couldn't help but admire the picture he made.

"Well," said Brad, interrupting her thoughts. Embarrassed to have been caught staring at him, she sank back down onto the foot of the lounge. "You certainly seem to be on good terms with my father."

"Yes," she replied coldly. "He doesn't take after his son."

"That should be the other way around."

"What do you mean?" she asked, disconcerted to find that in that brief period of time she had begun staring again, remembering what it was to drown in the deep-blue depths of his eyes, to the feel the tickle of his mustache against the tenderness of her skin. It was demoralizing to realize that no matter how furious he made her he could still affect her this way.

She was glad to have Brad interrupt her wayward thoughts. "You said that he didn't take after me. The son should take after his father."

"He certainly should!" she agreed enthusiastically, twisting his lesson in semantics to suit her own purpose. "Unfortunately, in this instance, that's not the case."

"Here we are, Brad," said Robert, interjecting himself into what had all the makings of an incipient brawl. He handed his son his drink and reseated himself beside Katherine, even though there were other chairs available.

Brad took a deep swallow of his drink. "So," he said with deceptive amiability, "what little plot have the two of you been hatching up this afternoon? Trying to figure out a way to push me into this marriage-merger scheme of yours?"

He couldn't have found a better way of killing Katherine's fantasies about him, fantasies she was all too happy to forget. "Why, you, you . . ." she said furiously. "I told you, I withdrew my offer. I wouldn't marry you now if you begged me!"

"Don't hold your breath," Brad advised callously. For some reason it appeared that just looking at her brought out the ire in him, as though witnessing the comfortable companionship she shared with his father roused him to fury.

Before Katherine could overcome her indignation long enough to give him another blast from the sharp edge of her tongue, Robert had stepped in.

"Now, now, children," he said appeasingly. "There's no point in all this squabbling. And as for you, Brad, you needn't think that there's any scheme against you afoot. There was never any intention to force you into something you had no taste for, but when Katherine came to me telling me that her engagement to Harold Hastings was at an end, well, I was naturally concerned for her because of the peculiar way her father framed his will. I'd hate to see her lose Hastings, when she's done such a fine job of running it. Anyway, for one reason or another, it occurred to me that you might want to make it possible for her to activate option three of the will. That's all there was to it."

"That sounds so damned innocuous the way you put it," Brad remarked with distaste, "when what it actually come down to is that you want me to play the part of some high-priced stud!"

"Stop saying that!" Katherine screamed.

Robert put a restraining hand on her shoulder as though he were afraid she might physically attack his son. "Brad," he reprimanded his son, "I'd appreciate it if you'd watch your language when you're in the presence of a lady."

"Watch my language!" Brad stormed in protest. "That's a good one. That *lady* could swear the pants off a sailor! Besides which, I think my summing up of the situation was pretty close to the mark."

"You're offended by the proposition?" his father asked him.

"Yes! No! Hell, I don't know!" Brad fumed as he threw down the rest of his drink. "I wasn't particularly at first, but then...Let's just let it drop, shall we? It may have originally been your idea, Dad, but now it's between Katherine and myself, and I think we should discuss something else."

Seemingly not in the least put out by his son's brusqueness, Robert regarded him calmly. "I'm afraid we can't do that. As I'm sure Katherine told you, she has one year from the time of her father's death to make up her mind which option she was going to choose. It's now been over eleven months and something will have to be done soon. She tells me that despite your objections you did not flatly turn her down."

"I told you I didn't want—"

"Be quiet, Katherine," said her uncle. Katherine was shocked. Never before could she remember her uncle having spoken to her so sternly.

"Was the proposition so distasteful to you that you refuse even to consider it?" he said pressing Brad for an answer.

"I told her I'd think about it."

"And have you?"

"I'm still thinking."

"And how long do you think it will take you?"

"How should I know?"

Robert shrugged. "I wouldn't have thought it such a difficult decision to make. After all, she's a lovely young woman, and she's got brains, too. She'll make some lucky man an excellent wife."

Katherine could take no more. Despite an attempt on

her uncle's part to prevent her, she jumped to her feet. "And I have all my own teeth, too," she snapped. "Really, Uncle Robert, you don't have to enumerate my good points as though I were some heifer standing on the auction block. And since neither of you seems to have been listening, I'll tell you again—I have withdrawn my offer. I wouldn't marry you now on a bet!" She glared at Brad.

"And I told you—" Brad began, only to be interrupted by his father.

"Stop it, both of you. You're acting like children. Now, sit down and behave yourselves."

Having been properly chastised, they both sat back down but continued to glare at each other across the short space separating them.

"Now," Robert said reasonably, "if you can do so without yelling, suppose you explain your position in all this, Brad."

Brad ran a hand restlessly through his hair, reminding Katherine once again of how she had so passionately rearranged that very head of hair just a few short days ago. "It's quite simple," he snapped. "She asked me to marry her and I told her I'd think about it. Surely every prospective bride is allowed some time to think it over," he added venomously.

"And I told him he could stuff it!" Katherine countered inelegantly.

"And if I do, just what the hell are you going to do about fulfilling the terms of that damned will?"

"I'll marry someone else, that's what I'll do!" Katherine told him with false bravado. Actually she had no idea what she was going to do, but she wasn't about to tell him that.

"That's a very good idea!" Brad taunted.

"You think I can't? You think I can't find someone else to marry me?"

Once more Robert intervened.

"This argument is totally pointless," he told them. "If you don't want to marry Katherine, Brad, that's fine. She won't lose out on her inheritance. Before I let that happen, I'll marry her myself."

CHAPTER FOUR

BOTH KATHERINE AND Brad sat staring at Robert as though he had suddenly grown two heads. Brad was the first to find his voice. With an unconvincing laugh he said, "You're kidding!" When he got no reply he exclaimed, "Of course you are! You've got to be joking!"

Slowly Robert shook his head. "Do you really think I would stand idly by and watch Katherine lose everything she's worked for, just because of some unfortunate clause in her father's will?"

For a long moment there was silence, the younger pair of the trio staring in shocked disbelief at their elder relative. Again it was Brad who broke the silence. "Ah, yes, the will." A smile spread across his face, the first in quite some time. "If you stop and think for a moment, you just might recall that there is another very important provision in that will. Not only must she marry by the specified date, she must also produce an heir within three years after her marriage."

Robert raised an eyebrow in query, so very much like the expression favored by his son that Katherine's breath caught in her throat. She was beginning to feel as though she had fallen down the rabbit hole as she heard Robert calmly say "So?"

"So the most you could hope to do is buy her three years."

"And that would be three years she won't have if she doesn't marry at all. As for that being the end of it, only time will tell."

"What do you mean by that? If she doesn't . . ." The smile froze on Brad's face. The air went out of him in a rush, as if he had just received a punch to the midsection. "You're not serious," he said at last. "You can't be serious." Jumping to his feet, he paced across the patio, and for a moment Katherine thought he was leaving. But suddenly he whirled on his heel and stalked angrily back to stand menacingly before his father. "Good God, man," he exclaimed through clenched teeth. "You're old enough to be *my* father," he said, his voice heavy with irony.

A smile of amusement lit his eyes as Robert reached out to pat his son on the shoulder. "Son, I *am* your father and nothing will ever change that. But that doesn't mean I can't be someone else's father as well. As for the difference in our ages, that's not so unusual."

Putting his arm around Katherine's shoulders, he gave her a squeeze. "There're any number of cases where such May-December marriages worked out excellently. How about Bing Crosby and Katherine Grant? Another Katherine." He laughed, giving Katherine another squeeze. "They had not one child but three and were apparently a devoted couple until the day he died."

Brad stood staring at his father. The men were tall and good-looking, the one a younger, more rugged version of the older. They stared into each other's eyes, both the deep blue of the sea, but while the elder's reflected a calm amusement, the younger's resembled the wave-tossed turbulence of the storm raging within him. At last the calm exploded as Brad turned to his father furiously. "But that would make her my stepmother!" he shouted.

"So what?" Robert asked, coolly rational, seemingly not the least disturbed by the passionate response his actions were obviously creating in his son. If anything, he looked inordinately pleased with himself. "What possible difference could that make? I'm sure we can trust Katherine's good sense not to try mothering you. And as you're apparently not interested in marrying her yourself, I fail to see how it concerns you."

"Ah-ha!" Brad exclaimed. "So that's the deal, is it? This is the little scheme the two of you have cooked up to force me into marrying her. Well, it won't work. When and if I decide to marry, it will be because it's what I want to do, not because of some damned will or because someone tricked me into it!"

Until this point Katherine had done little more than stand open-mouthed watching the tableau being played out by the two men in front of her. But upon Brad's unjustified accusation she came to life with a vengeance. "Why, you egotistical toad! You've got your nerve! No one's been cooking up any scheme to force you to give up your carefree existence, your free-wheeling bachelorhood. I told you the other night, I told you again today, I withdrew my proposal!"

Brad's attention had mainly been focused on his father,

but now he turned to Katherine. "And I told you that I won't allow you to withdraw the offer until I've had time to come to a decision."

"Save yourself the trouble. There's no point in over-taxing your limited powers of concentration to no good purpose. I would rather marry the poodle next door than marry you!"

"Oh, yeah!" Brad taunted.

"Yeah!" Katherine responded, her chin stuck out aggressively.

Neither of them noticed Robert, who had taken a step or two backward, giving them the floor. His hand covered his mouth, but nothing could disguise the merriment dancing in his eyes as he watched them behaving like a pair of undisciplined children.

"The poodle next door or my father!" Brad stormed.

"That's right!" Katherine answered defiantly. Her feet were firmly planted, her hands on her hips, her full breasts rising with the exertion of her anger. The color in her cheeks was heightened, her brown eyes snapping with indignation as she continued to rage at him. "The poodle would be an improvement over you. There's no comparison with your father!"

"Is that right?" Brad asked furiously as he stepped across the narrow space separating them. Before she sensed what he was about to do, Katherine felt his hands firmly on her shoulders. There was no time to protest as he jerked her against the solid wall of his chest, knocking the wind out of her.

While she was still stunned and gasping for breath, his mouth covered hers in a long hard kiss of frustrated arrogance. When he at last released her, his expression had not softened by one whit. "That," he jeered, "should give you something to think about, Mommie dearest.

You'll be hearing from me." And with that he turned on his heel and left them, not even glancing at his father before slamming the gate and stomping down the sidewalk.

With the squealing of Brad's tires dying in her ears, Katherine turned uncertainly to her uncle.

"I'm sorry about that, Katherine," he soothed. "He was upset."

"Yes," Katherine responded automatically. "But not entirely without reason." She would rather be staked out on an anthill than admit as much to Brad himself, but thinking about it without his disturbing presence, she could understand his chagrin.

Robert shrugged his shoulders. "Perhaps."

"Oh, I don't think there's any question about it. He makes me absolutely furious, but I can see his point. I'm sure he feels that we're putting pressure on him, trying to force him to marry me when he doesn't want to, when actually there's nothing I want less. Never was it my intention to try to coerce anyone into marrying me, regardless of the terms of my father's will or the fact that I stand to lose a great deal of money if I don't marry."

Robert patted her shoulder. "I know that, my dear."

"But Brad doesn't. He thinks I was in on your plot to try to force him to marry me by offering yourself as a substitute, and while I appreciate your motives, I really wish you hadn't done it. I think it would be best if you went home and explained to him that it was all a joke, and if possible try to get it through that thick head of his that I am not panting to marry him or anyone else."

"Not even the poodle next door?" Robert queried in amusement.

The ridiculousness of the situation struck Katherine, and she laughed at her own foolishness. "Not even him."

She laughed again. "Actually I think it's a her instead of a him."

Robert threw back his head and roared with laughter; the gesture was very like Brad's. "That makes it even more improbable," he agreed.

"Not much more improbable than my marrying you. I can't believe Brad took you seriously."

Robert gave her a look of feigned anguish. "I think I'm insulted. You told Brad you preferred me over the poodle. Have you changed your mind?"

Katherine grinned as she dropped down on the lounge once more and reached for her glass. "It seems I am continually telling Brad things I don't necessarily mean," she admitted ruefully.

"Now I *know* I'm insulted," Robert told her. "I mean, come on, Katherine. Surely I'm preferable to a poodle, a female one at that!"

"Depends," she teased. "Preferable for what?"

Robert stood looking down at her. Slowly he shook his head. "I don't know whether to envy my son or feel sorry for him. He's going to have his hands full."

Katherine felt the color rise in her cheeks. "I don't know what makes you say that. I've said I changed my mind about wanting to marry him."

"And pigs can fly, too." Robert snorted derisively. "I've always known that the two of you would be perfect together."

"Perfect together!" Katherine exclaimed. "How can you say that? Didn't you see the way we fight?"

"Yes, and I also saw the way you kiss. Both result from passionate feelings, just different sides of the same coin."

"I can't believe you," Katherine said angrily in a wasted

effort to camouflage what she was feeling, what she didn't want to recognize. "You act as though it's a *fait accompli* that Brad and I will marry, when in all probability I'll never see him again."

"I wouldn't worry about that." Robert smiled complacently. "He'll be back."

"And you think that's all it will take? He comes back and I fall gratefully into his arms and we live happily ever after? Is that the scenario? Is that the way you see it?"

Ruefully Robert shook his head. "Maybe that's how it happens in fairy tales, but in this case I'm sure you're both going to fight it every step of the way. I just hope you don't behave so foolishly as to jeopardize your position regarding your father's will."

In an attempt to lighten his mood, Katherine smiled and said, "Does this mean you're withdrawing your proposal? Are you so put out over the poodle that you're reneging?"

Slowly Robert shook his head. "No, I'm not reneging. If you two young fools can't get yourselves straightened out in time, I may have to step in at the last minute to save your inheritance."

Katherine couldn't believe he seriously meant what he was implying. "But you're my uncle!" she protested.

"Not really. I was once married to your aunt, that's all. We don't have a drop of common blood. So with that threat hanging over your head, I suggest you get cracking and make your peace with my son."

As he walked away she was almost in a state of shock. Never in her wildest dreams could she have imagined such a situation developing. It seemed years ago rather than one short week that she had been going about her normal routine, deeply engrossed in the running of her company and contemplating her marriage to Harold. The whole mythical dream had fallen apart when she had walked in on Harold and his secretary in very unbusinesslike circumstances. From that point on her entire life had been turned upside down.

CHAPTER FIVE

SHE ENTERED THE HOUSE, went upstairs, drew a long, hot bath, poured in the bubble solution with a generous hand, and sank gratefully into the tub. Still, she couldn't relax. She had a problem, a big problem. There was one short month, actually a little less than that now, to comply with the terms of her father's will. Otherwise, she would be out of Hastings on her ear. It was not that she was mercenary. She had always had enough money for what she wanted, and that fact would not change regardless of the outcome of the situation in which she now found herself.

As she had explained to Brad, her father had left his other holdings to her outright; in addition, she had managed to put aside quite a respectable sum on her own over the past few years. Her car and house were paid for; she could actually live comfortably if she never worked another day in her life. No, the problem was not money. The fact was that she did not want to give up her job. She liked it, she was good at it, and she would be bored out of her skull within a month if she were forced into a life of idleness.

After spending the evening watching a made-for-TV movie that was in its third or fourth rerun, Katherine had just taken the plate and glass from which she had eaten a meager meal back to the kitchen when the doorbell rang. Frowning, she looked down at herself. She had not been expecting anyone, and after taking her bath had put on her nightgown and robe.

The doorbell pealed again, and sighing, she pulled her dressing gown more closely around her and tightened the sash. It was a match to the very feminine gown she wore but at least it covered all of her respectably. She had washed her hair while bathing and brushed it out, letting it dry as she watched television, and now it hung, shining and dry, nearly to her waist. Impatiently she pushed it back behind her shoulders and went to answer the door.

Looking through the peephole, she felt her breath quicken and her heart rate accelerate as she saw Brad standing there, an impatient scowl on his face. Just as she reached for the doorknob he abandoned the bell to pound on the door with his fist.

"Katherine," he called curtly. "Open this door. I know you're in there, so don't try pulling anything."

Fumbling with the safety chain, she pulled the door open and glared up at him. "I do wish you would disabuse yourself of the notion that I am constantly trying to 'pull something' on you," she said self-righteously.

Not bothering to answer nor waiting for an invitation, Brad eased her aside, came in, and closed the door behind him. With only a sideward glance in her direction he stalked across the hall and down the two steps into her living room. Following, Katherine watched him go directly to the liquor cabinet, where he poured himself a stiff drink, raised it to his mouth, and took a deep swallow.

Moving down the steps Katherine stood watching him silently. "Help yourself, by all means," she said finally.

"Thanks, I just did. Can I get you anything?"

"How nice of you to offer, but no thanks, I don't care for anything just now. Maybe later, if you don't mind."

Entirely ignoring her biting sarcasm, Brad plopped himself down on the sofa, set his glass on the coffee table, pulled out his cigarette case, and lit up.

Katherine stood watching him, her feet planted firmly, her arms folded across her chest, her head cocked to one side. What in the world was he doing here? she wondered. After the way he had stormed off earlier in the day, she had thought she had seen the last of him. But now here he was, sprawled across her sofa, drinking her best Irish whiskey, and about to drop his filthy ashes on her carpet.

She bent forward and pointedly pushed the large, decorative ashtray across the table toward him. "If you must pursue that disgusting habit, I do wish that at least while you're in my home, you'd be a little neater about it."

"Damn, but you're a nag," Brad grumbled as he leaned forward to knock the ashes from his cigarette. "The man who marries you will have to be on his toes or you'll have him so henpecked he'll crow instead of saying good morning."

Katherine bristled. "Is that so?" she demanded imperiously.

"Yes"—Brad nodded—"that's so. If you're not careful, you're going to turn into a hardened, dried-up old maid by the time you're thirty."

"How dare you come in here and talk to me like that!" Katherine exploded. "No one invited you, and I certainly didn't ask for a character analysis!"

Brad grinned up at her as though appreciating the picture she made as he watched her through the smoky haze from his cigarette. And even in her anger Katherine couldn't help but be aware of his magnetism. Not that he was looking his best. He was still wearing the same pants and shirt he had been wearing that afternoon, but now they were rumpled and showing signs of wear. His hair was disheveled, as though he had not bothered to comb it since running his fingers through it so restlessly earlier in the day. His jaw was shadowed by the day's growth of beard, and he was altogether the best-looking man she had ever seen.

Katherine was shocked out of her detailed perusal of his appearance as he said, "That's what I like about you, Katie love, that sharp little tongue of yours and the mind behind it that gives it license to say such inflamatory things."

Katherine didn't know whether to be flattered or insulted. "I didn't know there was anything you liked about me," she retorted peevishly.

"Then that's where you were wrong," Brad murmured huskily as he let his wandering eyes take inventory of her feminine assets. "You've grown into a beautiful lady, Katie Hastings."

Katherine didn't quite know what to say, her sharp tongue and the mind that fueled it momentarily at a standstill. The best she could come up with was a stammered, "Th-thank you."

"That's all right," Brad told her magnanimously, and

for the first time Katherine noticed a slight slurring of his words.

"Have you been drinking?" she asked suspiciously.

"That's a silly question." He grinned crookedly. "Maybe you're not as smart as I thought you were."

"Never mind my IQ," she said, dismissing the taunt. "Just answer the question. Have you been drinking?"

"Not have, pretty lady, am," he explained as he lifted his glass to her in a mock salute.

"I can see that. Regardless of what you might think of my intelligence, there is nothing wrong with my eyesight, and even if there were, you would be a little hard to miss sitting there on my couch drinking my best whiskey."

Defiantly he downed the last of his drink, got up, and poured himself another. Carrying it back with him, he once more sprawled out across the sofa. Noticing the cigarette ash he had dropped down the front of his shirt, he very carefully brushed it off onto the carpet. "Don't be stingy," he told her in reference to her gibe about drinking her best whiskey. "It's a very unattractive trait in a woman."

Katherine's hackles rose, but she drew back at the last moment before telling him just what he could do with his narrow-minded chauvinism. "Brad," she said in exasperation, "what are you doing here? It's late and I want to go to bed."

"Sounds good to me." He leered at her.

In spite of herself, Katherine could feel the heat boiling in her bloodstream at the suggestive gleam in his eye, just now roving over her lightly clad body. "Alone, I want to go to bed alone," she said, her denial as much for her own edification as his. "So why don't you just say what you came to say, and then go?"

Brad shrugged and took another swallow of his drink. "I came to ask whether or not you were serious when you threatened to marry my father."

Sighing deeply, Katherine sank down on the sofa beside him. "I didn't threaten to marry your father," she told him with fraying patience. "Haven't you talked to him since leaving here this afternoon?"

Brad shook his head.

"And where have you been since you left here?"

Shrugging, he made his way to her liquor cabinet once again. "Oh, here and there," he replied carelessly. After refilling his glass he sat down beside her again, leaving much less space between them on the large sofa than before. He placed his glass on the table and pulled out another cigarette.

"Oh, no, you don't," Katherine asserted as she reached over him to pull the cigarette out of his hand. "You can drink my whiskey if you must, but I'm tired of you dropping ashes all over my carpet and furniture."

Unperturbed, he smiled. "Then I guess I'd better find something else to do with my hands, hadn't I?" His large hands spanned her waist, and before she knew what was happening she was sitting across his lap.

"Let me go, you big ape," she protested hotly as she struggled to free herself. "What do you think you're doing?"

"If you have to ask that," Brad said with a grin, "either I'm not doing it right or you're even more repressed than I thought."

She could have told him that he was wrong on both counts. She really hadn't needed to ask, and as for his technique, she didn't suppose he could "do it" wrong if he tried. She was fighting both of them as she struggled, opening her mouth to give him a blast of her temper. But her efforts were useless as his strong arms held her effortlessly, his hands restraining but gentle, his mouth very effectively shutting her up as it settled determinedly on hers.

The results were instantaneous, like two hot wires touching, sparking and crackling with electricity. Caught in a whirlpool of unadulterated passion, within a very short time Katherine had lost even the desire to struggle as she surrendered to the mindless rapture she had felt in the arms of no other man. She might spar with him, her tongue might try to flay his hide and cut his oversized ego down to size, but there was no denying that he could light a fire deep within her with even the lightest caress.

Not that what he was doing now could be described as lightly caressing, not by any sense of the words. As she had ceased to struggle, his hold on her had relaxed, his lips and hands now tempting and tantalizing rather than demanding.

And Katherine gave herself up to the temptation. In her rational mind she would have denied the possibility, but even the odor of too much alcohol on his breath mixed with the pungent tang imparted by the smoking habit she deplored, the musky smell of his body, and the almost painful rasp of his unshaven cheeks across her soft skin acted as an almost overwhelming stimulant to her senses. Her hands crawled up the broad expanse of his shirt front, pausing to test, to explore, the well-defined muscles beneath the rumpled material. Finding the corded strength of his neck and shoulders, her fingers kneaded and smoothed, and she was rewarded by the soft groan of pleasure that sounded somewhere deep in Brad's throat.

Soon Katherine was answering with soft breathless

moans of her own as his lips trailed fire along the line of her jaw, down the straining slender elegance of her throat to nibble hungrily at the smooth bareness of her shoulder so recently exposed by his questing fingers, his mustache brushing across her satin-smooth skin. Until she felt his mouth on her shoulder she hadn't realized that he had undone the sash of her robe or that he was attempting to slide it down her arms. Caught so quickly and completely by the web of the seductive spell he wove, she made no objection but pulled her arms free with one smooth motion, wrapping them tightly around him once again.

The world was spinning faster and faster, making her dizzy with the fever created by exploring hands and lips, the heat and hardness of his thighs beneath her, thrilling as they pressed into her soft underside.

"God, but you're gorgeous," Brad moaned as his eyes raked her very feminine form clad only in a revealing nightgown of amber satin and lace. Once again his mouth found hers and she gave him back feverish kiss for feverish kiss. When his mouth left hers she uttered a soft moan of distress, but then once again his lips were trailing fire across her face, down the length of her neck, to the delicious curve between neck and shoulder.

And, inexplicably, there he stopped. It took a long moment before she realized that there was something wrong. Her body was tensely arched, her head thrown back to give him easy access to her throat. She waited in breathless anticipation for his next move, the blood singing in her veins, her breasts swollen with excitement. But eventually, as nothing more happened, the tension relaxed and she looked down at his dark head cradled in the curve of her shoulder. As she felt his full weight slumping against her, she experienced a moment of panic.

What was wrong with him? Had he had a heart attack? She knew that it was not unheard of for this to happen to a man while making love, but surely it would take more than what they had done so far! And Brad was young, a man in his prime.

Then she heard it. At first she thought he was moaning, then to her shock and dismay she discovered that what she was hearing were not moans but snores! Brad was asleep.

She shook his shoulder. "Brad, Brad, wake up. What do you think you're doing?"

Her only answer was a loud snore as his head lolled back on his neck.

"And I guess that answers that," she told herself dryly.

Giving his upper body what support she could, she crawled off his lap, then let him sink down onto the sofa. For a long moment she stood looking down at him, his feet still on the floor, one arm dangling down with his hand resting on the carpet, his lips slightly parted as his deep breathing gave testimony to his sleeping state.

"So what do we do now?" she asked no one in particular. Once again she leaned over and shook his shoulder. "Brad, Brad, wake up. You've got to go home. You can't stay here." Once again her only answer was a slight change in his breathing pattern.

"Then, on the other hand, maybe you can," she remarked ruefully as she took one of the throw pillows and slid it beneath his large, handsome head. Getting his legs up and stretched out was more of a problem. Each one was as big as a log, and even while she struggled to lift them, putting her arms around them, feeling them pressed against her body, her pulse stirred and her breath came more quickly, and not just from exertion.

Once she had him stretched out and was standing

looking down at him, she had to admit to herself that even lying there in a drunken slumber, his mouth hanging open, his face needing a shave, his clothing soiled and wrinkled, he was still the most devastatingly appealing man she had ever known. Sighing, she bent over and removed his shoes, then went to get a blanket to cover him.

"It's a good thing I bought this overlong couch, Mr. Donovan," she told his sleeping form, "or you'd wake up in the morning with one hell of a crick in your neck." She chuckled softly to herself. "And if I'm not mistaken, you're going to have enough to contend with when you wake up as it is."

With that she switched off all but one small light, lest he wake up and wonder where he was, picked up her discarded robe, and made her way up the stairs to her lonely bed.

Once there, she lay flat on her back, her arms crossed above her head. What, she wondered, had Brad been doing here this evening? Then she felt the heat rising to her cheeks as she lay alone in the darkness. Actually she knew what he had been doing once he had gotten there, but what she didn't know was why he had come in the first place. When he had stormed out that afternoon she thought she'd seen the last of him. He had been quite furious, both with her and with his father. But now he lay sleeping peacefully in her front room. It was a puzzling situation and she was looking forward to his explanation in the morning. In the meantime, she rather liked the idea of knowing he was so near. With that thought, she sighed, rolled over, hugging her pillow to her, and went to sleep.

CHAPTER SIX

WHEN KATHERINE WOKE the next morning it took a long moment before she realized why she was feeling so light-hearted. Then she remembered. Brad was downstairs. And it was time for an explanation. She jumped out of bed, had a quick shower, and was dressed for work, all in record time.

She wore a tan silk two-piece suit with a scarf of white, gold, and brown at her neck. Her hair was once again pulled back into the smooth chignon she favored for the office. She slipped her stocking-clad feet into a pair of brown sling-back pumps, picked up the matching purse, and headed out of the bedroom door.

At the top of the stairs she slowed her pace. All right, she told herself, just play it cool. Act as though his being here is no big deal, as though you're quite used to having your couch occupied by devastatingly handsome men overnight. Don't let him see how strongly affected you are by him or that it was a struggle not to crawl in beside him rather than doing the sensible thing and going to sleep in your own bed. And whatever you do, put a curb on that sharp tongue of yours. He'll be embarrassed enough as it is and it probably wouldn't take much to send him on his way for good.

Her head held high, a welcoming smile on her face, she put one hand on the bannister and glided down the stairs with an air that would have done honor to a top-flight model. Unfortunately all her efforts were wasted because there was no audience to appreciate them.

She went directly into the living room, her eyes riveted on the back of the couch, but when she got to where she could see over the back, what she saw was her blanket neatly folded with a piece of paper on top of it.

Her shoulders slumped; her sophisticated pose evaporated as quickly as the dew in the desert sun. Disgruntled, she walked across the floor and picked up the paper. The writing was sharp and precise. So was the message, even though she did not understand exactly what it portended. It said simply: "Katherine, We have to talk. I'll be in touch. Brad."

"And just what the hell is that supposed to mean?" she asked the empty house. Kicking at her slippers— apparently they had come dislodged during the time spent on the sofa with Brad—she stomped into the kitchen, put bread in the toaster, and poured herself a cup of coffee from the coffeemaker that was programmed to come on at the same time her alarm went off.

Sitting at the table eating her spartan breakfast, she wondered again what Brad's cryptic note had meant. What did he want to talk about, and when would he be in touch? Was it possible that he had decided to marry her after all? And if he had, what would be her reaction? Weighing the pros and cons, she decided that she didn't want him to marry her out of a sense of duty or out of the fear that she might marry his father if he didn't perform this duty himself. She didn't want him to feel forced. If he agreed to marry her, she wanted it to be because that was what he really wanted to do.

And yet, time was flying by. In three weeks she had to have a husband or lose her claim to Hastings Electronics. She might not have the leisure to pander to his masculine sensibilities or to her own generosity of spirit and sense of fair play.

Later that morning, as she was sitting at her desk, Katherine looked through a contract requiring Hastings to furnish the electronic components for a government project. It was not big as government projects go, but at least it was a foot in the door. If Hastings did well on this one, they might get bigger and better government contracts in the future. There had been a number of companies bidding on it, Donovan's for one, and she was more than pleased that she had gotten it.

She was smiling as her secretary came in with the mail. "Good morning, Elizabeth," Katherine greeted her. "And how are you this morning?"

"Great!" the bubbling little brunette enthused. "And from the looks of it, I'd say the world is treating you right this morning, too."

Katherine smiled and acknowledged that it was true. She was pleased with the contract she was holding in her hands, and she had hopes for her personal life as well. The more she thought about Brad's message, the more she felt he must be about to tell her he wanted to marry her. One thing she was sure of, he just plain wanted her, and while last night might not be the best basis in the world on which to build a marriage, it was at least a start.

But the following day brought doubts. The sky appeared to be the limit as far as the growth and expansion of the company she headed were concerned, but it was beginning to look very much as though her personal life was headed for a dead end. She had foolishly let herself read too much into Brad's curt note. He had said they had to talk, that he would be in touch. She had had her ear half cocked all day for a message from him, but none had come. She had gone home telling herself that she had been foolish. Of course, he wouldn't call her at the office. She would hear from him that evening, but even though she had nearly sat on top of the phone the whole evening, it had refused to ring.

Two evenings later the phone did ring and Katherine was upon it before it had finished ringing once. She forced herself to stand beside it until it had rung six times. She did not want to appear too eager. Then suddenly panicking for fear he might hang up, she answered breathlessly, only to be greeted by her uncle. They spoke of nothing but small talk and business. No mention was made of deadlines or missing sons. Katherine wanted desperately to ask just where the hell Brad was and what the hell did he think he was doing, but she didn't.

It was late Friday afternoon when her secretary buzzed to say that Paul Hart from the accounting department would like to have a word with her. "Did he say what it was about, Elizabeth?" Katherine asked. Frowning, she noticed that it was now nearly six and that her secretary was on overtime, getting out the last of the letters that had been dictated that afternoon.

"He said he preferred to talk to directly to you,"

Elizabeth's voice said over the intercom.

Katherine sighed. It had been a long day, a long week, and she wanted nothing more than to go home and submerge herself in a hot bath. Nevertheless, she said, "Very well, send him in. But first, have you finished those letters that needed to go out tonight?"

"Just this minute," came the reply, and Katherine could hear the relief in her secretary's voice. It was Friday night and Elizabeth would be eager to get home to go out with her fiancé.

Katherine found herself feeling envious. It must be nice to be able to leave your work behind you, to worry about nothing more than having a good time. "Then bring them in first," she told Elizabeth. "The envelopes, too. I'll sign everything and get it in the mail. You can go on home."

She was sitting back in her chair, tired, and feeling a bit sorry for herself, when Elizabeth came in. "You look tired," Elizabeth said. "Why don't you just sign these and let me get them off for you. I can tell Paul to come back another time."

Katherine smiled wearily as she rolled her chair forward and began signing the letters before her. She shook her head. "No, that's all right, you go on. And you might as well send Paul on in. He evidently thinks it's important."

Some minutes later Katherine looked up to see a young man standing in front of her desk. Naturally she had seen him before, but as he was in the accounting department she had very little contact with him. That was Harold's department and she had left him to it. She had enough to contend with without hanging over the shoulder of every department head on her staff.

The young man named Paul Hart stood silently before

her, a shy smile on his face. He was twenty-three, had been on the Hastings staff for six months, was unmarried, and had a good potential for advancement.

"Won't you sit down?" Katherine offered politely as she glanced up from signing her correspondence. "I'll be with you in just a minute."

The young man sat on the edge of the chair in front of her desk. "That's all right," he said diffidently. "I don't mind waiting."

Katherine smiled and went on with her work, at the same time aware of the young man sitting across from her looking as though he were afraid she might bite. Was she really so formidable? She was only two years older than he; was it her position that made her so intimidating?

When she had signed the last envelope she looked up at him and smiled brightly. "And now what can I do for you, Paul?" His face reddened and he ran a finger around the inside of his collar. "It is Paul, isn't it?" she asked, fearing for a moment that she had gotten the name wrong.

"Yes, Miss Hastings, it is, and, er, I want to thank you for taking the time to see me."

"No problem." She smiled, waiting expectantly.

Under the intensity of her scrutiny he again ran a finger around the inside of his collar. "I really don't know where to begin," he admitted sheepishly.

Oh, Lord, Katherine thought to herself. Just what I need at the end of a long day. None of her displeasure showed on her face, however, as she smiled encouragingly and said, "They say the beginning is always a good place to start."

His answering smile at what he apparently presumed to be a taste of her wit was a shadow of what a smile should be, and Katherine caught herself comparing it with the amused twitching of a shapely sensuous mouth peeking out from beneath a neatly trimmed mustache, an answering gleam shining in a pair of dark-blue eyes.

"This is extremely difficult for me," Paul told her, interrupting her straying thoughts.

"Somehow I got the feeling that it was." Katherine smiled ironically. "But I assure you that I don't bite. If you have something to say, I promise to listen with an open mind."

Paul sighed with relief. "Thank you, Miss Hastings, I really do appreciate this."

"Yes, so you've said. Now, in what way may I help you?"

The young man looked at her as though he wasn't sure whether she was upbraiding him, and Katherine suddenly felt ashamed of herself. "I really do want to hear what you have to tell me, Paul." She smiled encouragingly.

Paul looked relieved. "Well, I don't know whether or not you're aware of it, but I came to work here several months ago."

"Yes, I know." Katherine smiled. "We feel that you have a great deal of potential and we're expecting great things from you in the future," Katherine assured him, and if the look on his face was anything to go by, he was her slave for life.

"Oh, Miss Hastings, you don't know how much I appreciate having you say that. It makes what I have to do so much easier."

Katherine smiled, just wishing he would get on with it. "I'm glad, Paul, and now suppose you tell me just what this is all about."

"Yes, well, as you know, I came to work in the accounting department six months ago. At first I didn't notice anything out of line, I mean it takes a while to get used to a company's particular system. Not everyone does everything the same way, but as I got used to the way things were being handled, well, it just didn't seem right."

"What didn't seem right, Paul?" Katherine asked, a tremor of apprehension creeping up her spine.

"The way the books were being kept, some of the discrepancies I found."

"All of our accounts are programmed into our computer system, aren't they?"

Upon his confirming nod, she indicated the computer console on her desk. "Suppose you show me what you mean, Paul."

An hour and a half later Katherine understood exactly what was worrying her junior accountant. Something was definitely amiss. "Have you mentioned this to anyone else?" she asked.

At his negative reply she said, "Not even Mr. Hastings?" Again he shook his head. "Why not?"

While talking about his work, the young man had acted like an entirely different person, someone who knew what he was doing, but now he began to look uncomfortable again. "Well, actually I really hate to make any accusations, but I couldn't see how there was any way he wouldn't have known about it."

Katherine took a moment to absorb what he was implying. If there was a discrepancy, Harold knew about it, was in all probability responsible. She felt the weight of the world descend onto her shoulders. Even though she had discovered his faithlessness on a personal level, she would never have thought to suspect him of dishonesty when it came to handling company funds. Her father had brought him into the company right out of school and had made him an intrinsic part of the business, even making him a beneficiary in his will. Surely he wouldn't repay all of that by stealing from them. And yet, according to what she had just been shown, it looked very much as though that was exactly what he had been doing.

"How long have you suspected this?" she asked wearily.

"I've had my suspicions for some time. I've been pretty sure of them for the last six weeks or so."

"Why did you wait until now to bring it to my attention?"

Paul's self-assurance began to ebb once again as he became unable to meet her eyes. "To tell you the truth, I didn't know what I should do," he confessed. "I mean, everyone knew the two of you were engaged, and well . . ."

His voice trailed off, but it was unnecessary for him to go on. Katherine understood what he was saying. How could he have come to her with such a story about her fiancé? "And you've since learned that we are no longer engaged?"

At his affirmative nod, Katherine sighed and said, "Well, I'm very glad you've brought it to my attention now. I'll deal with it."

"How do you plan to handle it?" he asked, then flushed red with embarrassment at his presumption. "What I mean is, what I've shown you tonight doesn't prove anything conclusively. There's always the possibility that I've made a mistake somewhere, although, quite truthfully, I don't know where that could possibly be."

"Unfortunately neither do I," Katherine said wryly. "But in any case, I have no intention of slinging accusations right and left. That's a good way to bring a stiff lawsuit down on your head. No, Monday morning I will get in touch with a reliable audit company and they'll give all of our books a thorough going-over. If what we suspect is true, I'll decide the best way to handle it then."

Paul smiled a little uncertainly. "Well, I guess that's that then," he said as he stood up.

Katherine stood, too, noticing that in her heels she stood an inch or two taller than he did. "I want you to know I do appreciate what you've done, Paul. I know there's an old saying to the effect that the bearer of bad news comes in for his share of the blame, but I assure you that's not true in this case. I really do thank you."

The young man seemed to be having trouble coping with a combination of pride and embarrassment. "Oh, that's all right, Miss Hastings," he assured her enthusiastically. "I mean, I'm only too glad to do anything I can to be of help to you. I can't tell you how much I admire you, running a company this size, and you can't be more than five or six years older than me."

"Two years, actually," Katherine remarked dryly, then smiled to show him that she hadn't taken offense at his guessing her to be older than she really was.

"I'm sorry," he apologized. "It's hard to believe you're only twenty-five." Then he seemed to realize that his words could be seen as less than complimentary. "Not that you look any older," he hastened to assure her. "It's just so amazing that you have accomplished so much while being so young. I didn't mean to offend you."

Suddenly the funny side of the situation struck Katherine. She laughed and picked up her purse, then walked around her desk to take his arm, and began walking toward the door. "I'm not in the least offended, Paul," she told him brightly. "And just to prove it, I'm going to take you out to dinner to thank you for what you've done. You will come, won't you?"

His eager acceptance caused Katherine's spirits to lift. At least there was someone willing to have her company.

In the basement garage she directed him toward her car. "I thought we'd go to Antoine's if that's all right with you," she said, smiling as they got in. "My treat, of course," she added quickly as she noticed his face blanching. "I insist." She smiled, settling herself behind the wheel and turning the key.

Whether it had been his intention to argue or not, Katherine never knew, her attention being centered on her car and what it was not doing, which was starting. "Damn!" she retorted in disgust, pounding on the steering wheel with the palm of her hand.

"Do you know what's wrong with it?" Paul asked in amazement. It was as though he found it impossible to believe anything could go wrong with such a beautiful machine.

Katherine shook her head. "It's been a little sluggish lately, not starting as easily as it should, but this is the first time it's ever failed to turn over. I've been meaning to get it checked but never took the time. Do you think you might be able to do something with it?" she asked hopefully.

"I can sure give it a try," he said with the most enthusiasm and assurance he had displayed since walking into Katherine's office earlier that evening.

He got out of the car and lifted the hood. "Would you look at that!" he exclaimed.

"Have you found it already?" Katherine asked in surprised relief as she got out of the car and walked toward him.

"What? Oh, no," he replied with embarrassed chagrin. "It's just that I've never seen under the hood of one of these babies before. It's fantastic."

"It would be even more fantastic if it would run," Katherine commented dryly.

"Oh, yes. Well, we'll just have a look," he told her as he set to work.

Katherine stood at his shoulder watching as he poked and prodded at the mysterious innards of her car. "Can you see anything?" she asked without a great deal of optimism. This just hadn't been her day, her week in fact, and it seemed only fitting that it should end in such a miserable manner. If she hadn't already invited Paul to have dinner with her, and if he had not accepted with the enthusiasm of a friendly puppy, she would have called it a night and taken a cab home.

"Not yet," Paul replied to her question. Minutes slid by. "Here's your trouble!" he announced triumphantly. "The battery's out of water. I think you've probably ruined it."

Katherine's shoulders slumped. "That's just great," she said unhappily. "Now what do I do?"

She hadn't really been appealing to Paul for an answer to her problem but he seemed to think she was and appeared uncommonly flattered by the notion. "No problem," he assured her. "We can take my car this evening and you can call the garage tomorrow to replace your battery. I'm parked in the lot across the street. Let's go back upstairs and you can wait while I go get the car."

Katherine had been standing on the sidewalk in front of the Hastings building only a few minutes when she heard the roar of a motor that sounded like a small jet plane about to take off. She looked up to see Paul pulling up in front of her in a fire-engine-red sports car that seemed to sit directly on the pavement. When he reached over and pushed the door open for her, she stood contemplating the size of the door, the car, and her own long legs. "Where's the shoehorn?" she asked, smiling.

Paul laughed self-consciously. "It's easier to get in if you turn your back to it and sit down, then swing your legs up and around. There's actually plenty of room once you're inside."

Following his directions, Katherine found his last statement to be an optimistic exaggeration. The bucket seat was not uncomfortable, but most of the leg room was straight ahead under the long, impressive hood of the car. Her knees were higher than her bottom and her feet were stretched out so far in front of her that she could barely see them.

"Now, isn't that better?" Paul asked brightly.

Katherine wanted to ask, Compared to what? but couldn't because it would have been too much like slapping that friendly little puppy he so very much reminded her of.

CHAPTER SEVEN

IT WAS AFTER ten when Katherine again found herself sitting beside Paul in his flashy little car, holding on to anything she could find as they sped through the night.

She looked miserably ahead. Again she thought about what an awful week she'd had. And to top it off with a memorable finale, here she was sitting beside a young man, who was no doubt an eminently worthy person, but who only seemed to come to life with self-assertion when he found himself behind the wheel of this bright red bomb disguised as a motorized roller skate.

They had dined at Antoine's as planned, but in those surroundings Paul had acted totally out of his element. He had deferred to her in everything—choice of food, wine, even the placement of their table. And Katherine had made a surprising discovery about herself. She had always seen herself as a person who liked to take charge, and in her business affairs she was. She had found, however, that when the occasion was social, and particularly at the end of a rough day, it would have been a relief to have been able to leave the details of the evening to her escort.

Unbidden, another evening came to mind when she had taken another man out to dine. There had been no question on that occasion as to who was in charge. Despite his shortcomings, Brad was a man who got noticed, received prompt and efficient service, and didn't need to defer to anyone else's opinion.

When they roared to a stop in front of her house, Katherine didn't even try to suppress a sigh of relief. Paul got out and came around to open the door for her. He reached in and took her arm to help her out, help she was in no position to refuse. If left on her own, she might very well spend the rest of her life packed like a sardine into that little red can.

Once on her feet, she had to clutch at her escort's arm for a moment to get her balance. "Thank you, Paul," she said. "It's been quite an experience," she added with a twist of irony. "I've never ridden in a car quite like that before."

"She's really something, isn't she?" Paul asked, taking it for granted that she was impressed. "If you'd like, I can come get you and take you in to get your car tomorrow," he added eagerly. "Anytime. I wasn't going to be doing anything important."

"Oh, no!" Katherine said a little too quickly for politeness. Then, realizing that she might have hurt his feelings, she added, "I mean, thank you very much. That's very sweet of you, Paul, but the garage will deliver it once they have it running again."

"Oh, all right," Paul said, deflated. "Well then, I guess I'll just see you in."

There was nothing Katherine wanted more than to get rid of him, go inside her house, take two aspirin while filling the tub with gallons of hot soapy water, then submerge herself for the next two hours, but Paul looked so crestfallen that she relented. She really did owe him a great deal, and it wasn't his fault that he couldn't measure up to a certain tall, good-looking, exasperating gentleman who was never far from her thoughts.

Sighing to herself, she took Paul's arm and started toward her front door. "But you must come in and have a cup of coffee before going home so I can tell you again how grateful I am. Not just for your help this evening, but for what you told me back at the office. I do appreciate it, and know you won't let it go any further until after we have the auditors in."

They were actually almost ready to step up onto the front porch of her house when she looked up and saw a dark shadow detaching itself from its post beside her front door. The breath caught in her throat and she heard Paul gasp beside her, although, to do him credit, he did react automatically to push her behind him.

It was really very brave of him, but Katherine couldn't help but feel a bit foolish looking over the head of her knight as he stood his ground in the face of the unknown. In any case, there was no need for alarm as the shadow materialized and a well-remembered voice said, "Good evening, Katie love. Aren't you going to introduce me to your friend?"

Not waiting for her answer, he glided forward out of the shadows, seeming to tower over the two of them as though they were a pair of recalcitrant children. Placing a possessive arm around Katherine's waist, with his other hand he tipped her chin upward, and even as her intended protest caught unspoken in her throat, his mouth was on hers. His kiss was long and proprietary, as though he were asserting his rights of ownership even while ignoring the man who had been her escort.

Slowly withdrawing his mouth from hers, Brad looked deeply into her eyes, the light of the full moon reflecting a myriad of emotions, not the least of which was anger. But before she had a chance to revile him for the worm he was, for the anxiety he had caused her, and for embarrassing her in front of Paul, he was turning to smile at the younger man. "I hope you'll forgive us," he said affably, "but I've been away all week." As though that explained everything perfectly! Still clasping Katherine tightly against his left side, he offered his right hand. "I guess we'll have to introduce ourselves since the cat seems to have gotten Katie's tongue. I'm Brad Donovan, and you're..."

Paul seemed to be suffering from shock even greater than Katherine's, but he did at last manage to put his hand in Brad's, then instantly regretted it as it was engulfed in a punishing grip. "Paul Hart," he said through lips tightened with pain. "I work for Miss Hastings," he added for no apparent reason, almost as though excusing himself. "I brought her home. Her car wouldn't start."

"Really?" Brad asked, his eyebrow rising as though he were skeptical. But as quickly as the skepticism had registered, it was replaced with bland cordiality. "Then I owe you my thanks, and it's been a pleasure to have met you, Paul."

He was quite obviously dismissing the younger man, and Katherine found her temper rising by leaps and bounds at his high-handedness. But before she could blast him for the insufferable, conceited rat he was, Brad crushed her against the hard length of his body. In an apparently affectionate caress, his other hand captured her head, holding it captive against his broad chest. "I know you'll excuse us if we leave you now," he continued to Paul. "But as I said, I've been gone awhile, and we have a lot of lost time to make up for. If she weren't so overcome with emotion at seeing me again, I know my fiancée would want to thank you personally for seeing her home. These days you never know what might be waiting in the dark."

Ain't that the truth, Katherine wanted to say, but she couldn't because her mouth was buried against the front of Brad's jacket. She could hardly breathe, but when she did she was filled with the very essence of him, and she rediscovered that anger was not the only emotion that could make the blood rush through her veins.

"Your, your fiancée!" Paul exclaimed as he began to retreat. "I didn't realize. I mean, I had no idea, she didn't say . . ."

"That's my little Katie." Brad laughed good-naturedly. "Terribly shy about speaking up for herself. Then, too, our engagement's new to her and it takes her a while to get things straight in her mind," he explained as though she were a not very bright child who had difficulty with her lessons.

When Katherine made a choked croak into his shoulder, he laughed again before wishing Paul's receding back a cheerful good night.

As Paul took off in a streak of red fury, Katherine was partially released from her imprisonment, at least enough so that she found the use of her voice. "You—you despicable, overbearing . . ."

"Not here, Katie," Brad cautioned. "Let's have your key and we'll go inside."

"What makes you think I'd let you into my home now, you overgrown bully?" Katherine raged at him.

She had never been so incensed in her life, hadn't even known she was capable of such impassioned anger. If it hadn't been so laughably beyond her strength, she would have taken the greatest pleasure in beating him to a pulp.

"The key, Katie," Brad demanded as he held out his hand expectantly, totally unimpressed by her outburst.

Katherine glared at him impotently. In her anger she felt unable to deal with the hassle of searching her keys out of the bottom of her purse. Knowing, however, that it was useless to go on defying him, she turned to him grudgingly. "In the flowerpot by the door," she said, indicating where the spare key was kept.

"How original," Brad muttered as he went forward to look for the key.

Following him, Katherine ignored his sarcasm. "There's no point in your coming in," she affirmed stubbornly. "I don't want to talk to you. In fact, I never want to see you again!" A few days earlier it would have been a different story. If he had followed up on the implied promise in the note he had left her last Monday morning, everything could have been settled by now. But he hadn't followed up. He hadn't even bothered to call her the entire week. She had no idea where he had been or what he had been doing, and now if he thought he could waltz back into her life as though nothing had happened, he had another thought coming.

Brad found the key and opened the door. Turning aside to let her by, he smiled, saying, "It could be a bit difficult getting you pregnant under those circumstances, but it's up to you. I guess you could wear a blindfold. In any case, you're the boss, Katie."

The implication of his laughing remark, the mental picture of what he was suggesting, sent a tingling coursing through Katherine's veins, a burning sensation in the pit of her stomach. Unable to reply to the substance of what he was telling her, she vented her anger in another direction. With her head held high she preceded him through the door, turning lights on as she went. Passing him, she said furiously, "I've told you not to call me Katie! And since when did you ever give me the opportunity to be the boss of anything? Ever since I so stupidly invited you back into my life, you've tried to take over. Well, I won't stand for it, do you hear me?"

"Yes, my sweet, I hear you," Brad told her calmly as he guided her through the house into the living room. "And if you don't hold it down, they'll hear you next door, too."

When next she spoke her voice was lower but just as determined. "And another thing, just who the hell do you think you are, barging in like that? Telling Paul all those lies!"

Brad's brows drew together as though he were in pain. "I do wish you would stop swearing, my love. I've told you, it's so unattractive in a woman," he admonished her as he went to the liquor cabinet and poured them each a glass of brandy. "And as for your little friend, I thought I handled the situation very well."

"Very well! Telling him we're engaged, acting as though I were some sort of simpleton!" Glaring at him, she grabbed the glass he offered. "And I'll damn well swear if I want to!" she added for good measure as she unheedingly threw back her drink, coughing and sputtering as the liquid fire burned its way into her stomach.

"Need any help?" he offered politely.

"No," she gasped. "Not from you I don't." Turning her back to him, she fought for breath, her shoulders heaving, her eyes filling with tears.

Feeling Brad's hands on her shoulders, she tried to jerk away from him, but he was having no part of that. Turning her around and seeing the tears streaming down her cheeks, a look of remorse crossed his face. "Don't cry, sweetheart," he soothed her as he tenderly cradled her against him. "You know as well as I do that you really didn't want that poor boy who brought you home tonight. You'd eat him alive."

"What the hell are you talking about?" Katherine muttered indignantly as she pulled a handkerchief from the pocket of her skirt and began mopping at her face. She knew she was fighting to hold on to her righteous indignation, knew that it would be so very easy to succumb to the rare tenderness Brad was showing her, but she wasn't about to give him an easy victory. He owed her an explanation, a good explanation of just what he thought he was doing, where he had been, what he had meant by the note he had left her, and what he meant coming here tonight treating her the way he had. And saying the things he had to Paul.

Taking the handkerchief out of her hand, Brad gently dried her eyes. "I'm saying," he told her with restrained patience, "that he was no match for you. Though you try to deny it, there's fire in your veins. You're a very passionate woman, and you need a man who won't be intimidated by that side of your personality. Now, stop crying, honey, and admit that I'm right about that little boy you've been teasing all evening."

"I'm not crying because of that," Katherine admitted unthinkingly. "It's the damn brandy!"

She saw her mistake the moment the words left her mouth, for Brad greeted them with a bellow of laughter. If she'd been smart, she would have let him think whatever he wanted to. His version was at least more romantic than hers and had temporarily gained her his tenderness and sympathy.

On the last gasp of his laughter, Brad managed, "And I thought you were crying."

"I never cry," she told him as she lifted a determined chin, just daring him to contradict her. She didn't need his pitying condescension, she sternly reminded herself.

He cocked his head quizzically, but let her stubborn declaration pass unchallenged. "And you admit that Paul Who's-It isn't the man for you?"

"I didn't say that," she said stubbornly, even though she had been very much aware of that fact all evening. Paul Hart was a nice young man, and if he was correct in his findings regarding the company accounts, she was greatly in his debt. But there was no doubt in her mind that he was not the man for her. Possibly, had she wanted to pursue the matter, he could have been the instrument for meeting the requirements set forth in her father's will. She was not so blind as to be unaware of his admiration. But she couldn't bring herself to exploit his vulnerability.

"No, but you know it's true," Brad told her. "Really, love, I can't help being disappointed. I knew you'd find someone to throw in my face, but I did expect you to come up with someone a little more convincing than that hotrod adolescent. Surely, if you'd put just a bit more effort into it, you could have done better," he added amiably.

Katherine began to see the humor in the situation. And in any case, she really didn't want to fight him anymore. What she wanted was the explanation that was long overdue. "I was working against a deadline," she admitted with a rueful smile. "But you shouldn't laugh at Paul. He's hardly an adolescent and he's really very nice. He's intelligent, attractive—"

"You can stop right there, Katie," Brad interrupted imperiously. "I'm prepared to grant you a certain amount of latitude, but I don't intend to stand still while you reel off my rival's selling points."

"You have no rival."

A look of pleasant surprise crossed his face. "You flatter me, sweetheart." He smiled.

"You flatter yourself," she informed him dryly. "I only meant that there's no contest, that I've decided to accept the terms of the second option of my father's will." She really was not so fatalistic as she sounded, but as the deadline drew remorsefully closer she began to think the matter was slipping beyond her control. Besides, she had discovered at some point during her relationship with Brad that holding on to the control of Hastings was no longer top priority in her life.

"Now, let's see," Brad mused, seemingly unconcerned with the put-down. "That's the one where Cousin Harold walks away with the lion's share of your company. Really, Katherine, I thought better of you than that."

Katherine shrugged as she walked over and put her glass on the table, then sat down on the couch. "I don't seem to have much choice. It's either that or accept your father's generous offer, and I hesitate to do that even with the added inducement of making you my stepson into the bargain." She was deliberately baiting him, but damn it, he owed her an explanation and he was taking his own sweet time in offering it. He deserved to be made uncomfortable.

Brad scowled, all trace of amusement gone from his

face. "That's about the dumbest damn idea I ever heard of! You marrying my father! Why, it's indecent!"

"Well, it wasn't my idea," Katherine said, more than a little pleased with the reaction she had provoked. Then with a superb show of nonchalance she turned the screws a bit tighter. "And I certainly don't say I'd be willing to go along with it, but I don't see why you consider it indecent. As Robert said, we have no common blood. We're not actually related."

"So it's 'Robert' now, is it?" Brad sneered. "Whatever happened to the 'uncle'? It seems to me that you're not so set against the idea as you pretend to be."

"I'm not pretending anything. But in any case, I don't see that it's any of your business. Your father and I are both over twenty-one and we don't have to have your permission for anything we decide to do."

"One of you is considerably over twenty-one, and as for not needing my permission, I'm afraid you're mistaken."

"Don't be ridiculous!" Katherine declared, her temper flaring at his presumption. "Neither of us is obliged to ask you for anything, and if you mean to try to have your father declared incompetent, you're going to have a battle on your hands. Because I'll fight you tooth and nail." The entire argument was pointless, and Katherine knew it. She had no intention of marrying his father, but he put her back up with his dictatorial decrees. Besides, he had not made the least effort to explain where he had been this past week, why he hadn't called, and what he had meant by the note he had left her.

With a wave of his hand Brad dismissed her heated declaration. "Don't be a fool," he said scornfully. "I know as well as you do that my father is as mentally capable as he ever was, and even if he weren't, I'd never do something like that to him."

"Then what were you talking about? And don't call me a fool!"

"Then don't act like one. As for what I was talking about, I was referring to you, not my father. It's you who needs my permission."

"Now who's the fool!" Katherine exploded in disbelief. "You're not only a fool, you're just plain crazy! I don't have to answer to you for anything!"

"Oh, but you do," he assured her. "When you asked me to marry you, you granted me certain implied rights."

"I did no such thing!"

"Oh, but you did."

"That's the craziest thing I ever heard! And you're by far the craziest man I ever met! Just who the hell do you think you are?"

They had both been sitting on the sofa, one at each end and turned sideways to face each other, the electricity snapping between them with an almost tangible force. But Katherine's last statement had hardly passed her lips before Brad had eliminated the distance between them, his hands snaking out to capture her wrists in a steely grip. "That's the second time tonight you've asked me that, and it's time you had your answer," he growled, glaring down into her shocked eyes.

Before she could protest, he pulled her against him, releasing her hands so that he could wrap his arms tightly around her, holding her powerless against the bruising strength of his hard chest. Without further ado he lowered his head and his mouth plundered hers in a sweet but punishing kiss.

Leaving her breathless, he finally drew his head back.

"I'm the man you asked to marry you, that's who," he said with grim determination, "and now I'm ready to give you your answer."

His kiss had robbed Katherine of the breath and the desire to argue with him, but her heart leaped into her throat at what she was hearing and her eyes were eloquent as she waited for his next words.

Brad smiled lazily down into her eyes, accurately reading the anticipation he saw revealed. Tenderly his long fingers caressed her face. "All your dreams are about to come true, sweetheart," he said wryly. "I've decided to accept your proposal. Aren't you pleased? Just think, I'm yours for the taking."

"God, it boggles the mind!" Katherine exclaimed with a shuddering sigh, not knowing whether what she was feeling was relief, apprehension, or outrage that he had taken so long to decide, or was a result of the conceited, egotistical way he had gone about telling her of his acceptance.

"Doesn't it just?" Brad laughed, taking in her rueful exclamation. "Naturally at the moment you're overcome just thinking about your good fortune, but you'll learn to live with it."

Had he not treated it all as though it were a frivolous joke, Katherine would probably have accepted his decision without further protest. As it was, however, it distinctly rubbed her the wrong way, wounded her pride. How could he make so light of something she had come to realize meant a great deal to her? And not just from a business standpoint.

Her protest was automatic as she tried to battle against the temptation of sharing his infectious good humor, the warm proximity of his hard, unyielding body, the remaining tingle from the imprint of his lips against hers.

"I've told you," she said, deploring the weakness she recognized in her own voice, "I've decided to go with the second option."

He shook his head. "Now, don't be stubborn, Katherine." His hands caressed her back soothingly, sliding up the sides of her arms, curving around her shoulders. "You know very good and well that you forfeited that option when you asked me to marry you and give you my child. And, if you're honest, you'll admit that if I had given you my answer a week ago instead of making you wait, you would have been busily planning the wedding right now instead of doing a poor imitation of a prickly cactus."

"Well, why didn't you?" Katherine demanded unwarily, fighting the slow insidious seduction of his caress, forgetting her intention not to let him know how put out she had been by his apparent indifference.

"Not accept last week? But darling, I thought you would realize, it's modesty that makes us sweet little innocent men insist on time to think it over before committing our bodies..."

He was laughing at her and ineffectually, she struck out at him in frustration. But all she accomplished was to make him laugh harder, although he did capture her wrists in his hands to prevent any further physical retaliation. "You haven't got a modest bone in your body, Brad Donovan!" she ranted at him. "I don't know why in the world I ever proposed to you in the first place."

"I should think there were any number of reasons," he told her immodestly as he continued to smile down into her face. "First, there was the fact that you thought it would be easier to propose to someone you knew. Second, I am eminently eligible, my financial prospects are outstanding, and I'm sure to win approval of your trustees. And third, and probably most important, I'm passably good-looking and you lust after my body."

Katherine's face flared. "You certainly don't lack for conceit, do you?" she demanded, unable to honestly deny any of his contentions. Even though he was an egotistical oaf for having the gall to enumerate them.

The light of amusement dancing in his eyes, Brad shook his head. "It won't work, sweetheart."

"What won't work?" Katherine blustered. "I haven't the least idea what you're talking about."

"Oh, yes, you do," he said, contradicting her calmly. "I may have let on to that boy who brought you home tonight that you're not terribly bright, but we both know differently. You're sharp as a tack, with a tongue to match, but if you think you'll put me off with mockery and snide little digs at my ego, you're all out of luck. It just won't work."

The thought crossed Katherine's mind that she must look ridiculous practically lying in his arms, snapping at him like an angry cat, when all she really wanted to do was surrender to the magnetism that was the essence of the man. But still, she fought on. "All I'm trying to do is get it through that thick head of yours that I've changed my mind. I don't want to marry you!"

"Scared?" He grinned.

"Of course not! And I don't lust after your body!" she added for good measure.

He laughed softly, his eyes sparkling with amusement, the corner of his mustache twitching in a way that she had always found fascinating. He lowered his face to hers, his lips lightly caressing her cheeks, the tip of his tongue gently exploring the curves of her ear, his teeth nibbling delicately at the lobe. "I'll be more honest than you're being. I'll admit that I lust after you," he whispered huskily. "All this week I've thought of very little except you. I had an early plane to catch last Monday morning, and was out of town on business for the rest of the week. But I don't think I accomplished much. I couldn't get my mind off of you, of how it had been between us Sunday night. Oh, I know I had had too much to drink, but I wasn't so far gone that I didn't know what I was doing. And I've wanted to repeat the performance every minute of every day since."

The breath caught in Katherine's throat as she listened to his words. Her eyes were wide with wonder, her fingers hesitantly tracing the outline of his face. "Why didn't you call?" she asked unsteadily.

"Because I couldn't have said what I wanted to over the phone. I couldn't have felt you in my arms, seen the smoldering passion in your eyes."

While his lips continued to caress her face and throat, one hand went to her hair and began systematically removing the pins and throwing them carelessly on the floor. "As for not being afraid, I think you are. You're afraid of the way I make you feel." He began running his fingers through her loosened hair. "Afraid of the way you lose control when I make love to you."

It was all Katherine could do to continue denying the truth of what he was saying, fighting for self-control. A warm tingling weakness had begun to swamp her as his caresses became more and more erotic. She could stand up to his opposition, share or strike out against his humor, but his tender seduction was slowly but surely forcing her unconditional surrender. "You haven't made love to me, at least not fully," she said, her breathing labored. "And I certainly don't lose control," she added, struggling against making a liar of herself.

"Shall we see?" He grinned. As she shrank away from

him he laughed indulgently, effortlessly manipulating her senses. "You should be careful what kind of challenge you issue, sweetheart, because you have to know I'm going to take it up."

Tangling his fingers in her hair, he began pulling her toward him. "God, but you've got glorious hair. Let free it shimmers and shines like molten gold. I was shocked when I first saw it this way, Sunday night. All week I've remembered how it looked and wanted to see it that way again, wanted to bury my face in it, smell it, taste it." His actions followed his words, sending all kinds of erotic messages to the core of Katherine's womanhood, exciting compelling messages, the strength of which she had never felt before.

"Relax, honey," he gently coaxed her as she impotently held herself rigid in his arms, still fighting to regain a hold on sanity.

His lips softly brushed across hers, then followed the line of her jaw to her ear, where his tongue and teeth again teased and tasted. "Hmmm," he murmured. "You taste as good as you smell. I love that sexy perfume you wear."

Katherine felt herself surrendering, and blind instinct urged her to protest. "Don't . . ."

"Shhh. Don't fight it, darling," he urged. "Don't think, just feel." He brought his mouth back to hers, at the same time pulling her more comfortably into his embrace, cradling her head in the hollow of his shoulder, her long, unbound hair streaming over his arm.

His mouth warmly covered hers, his tongue began to slide along the sweet curve of her lips. A thumb pulled gently at her lower lip. Feeling the shiver that shook her entire body, he pressed home his advantage by deepening their embrace; and when his large hand settled warmly, possessively, over her full breast, her gasp was enough to allow further penetration of his tongue.

At this intimate invasion Katherine lost all hope of fighting him. Her hands had been trapped between their bodies, but she fought to free them, raising them to fiercely encircle his neck, her fingers restlessly raking through the fullness of his hair.

"That's it, sweetheart, let go." He groaned encouragement. "God, but I love it when you explode in my arms."

Through the blazing passion enshrouding her mind, Katherine realized that he wasn't saying that he loved her, only the way she responded to him, but even that knowledge couldn't temper the fire raging within her. Always she had held back, never surrendering completely to the passionate side of her nature, never exposing her vulnerability. Only this one man seemed able to ignite the smoldering embers deep within her, and he could do it with scarcely more than a touch. She had been right to try to put him at a distance once she had discovered the catastrophic effect he had on her. Now it was too late. She had innocently invited the vanquisher into her life, and the victory was his.

Mindlessly Katherine arched her neck as Brad's lips rained fire down its length to the frantically beating pulse at the base of her throat. There he paused, letting his tongue taste and absorb every frenzied beat of her heart, making it a part of him.

Katherine hadn't even been aware of the loosening of the zipper at the back of her dress, but even as she dimly realized what was happening, she offered no resistance as he slid the dress from her shoulders.

She lay in his arms across his lap, her dress bunched at her waist; and as he pulled back to look at her she could see the blistering passion in his eyes, feel the demanding desire of his manhood pulsing beneath her. "You're gorgeous," he moaned almost reverently as he drank in the sight of her, her hair free and wild, her eyes alive and dark with passion, her lips soft and vulnerable from his kisses.

He lowered his head to caress the soft, burgeoning curves of her breasts, his tongue tasting, worshiping their sweetness. "So white and soft," he moaned huskily. "So delicious."

Scarcely mindful of the fact that they had moved, Katherine found herself lying down, Brad's weight seductively pinning her to the couch. With his head buried in the valley between her breasts, his hand slid beneath her, pulling her closer, molding their lower bodies together, intriguing, if shocking, her with the extent and heat of his desire.

His other hand sought and found the back clasp of her bra. And though knowing his intention, she didn't fight him, but instead arched her back to give him easier access, sighing with relief when the bit of lace was dispensed with.

They were caught together in the whirlwind of their emotions, giving and receiving, oblivious of time and space, floating beyond the mundane considerations of reality. But even Paradise had its serpent, and in the far recesses of her mind Katherine became aware of a disturbance.

"Brad," she whispered breathlessly as she wrenched her mouth from his. "The doorbell's ringing. Someone's at the door."

"Ignore it and maybe they'll go away" was his callous advice as he again sought her lips.

As much as she would have liked to have followed

his suggestion, her conscience wouldn't let her. "I can't," she insisted. "It might be important. Let me up."

With obvious reluctance Brad rolled off her, giving her a hand to help her up. Without a word he turned her around, pulled her dress back into place, and zipped it up. Parting her hair, he placed a pulsating kiss at the nape of her neck. "Let's hurry and get rid of them," he murmured warmly.

Throwing her hair back over her shoulders, Katherine went to the door, aware that Brad was following her. Taking a deep breath to steady her racing heart, she opened the door.

CHAPTER EIGHT

"KATHERINE, ARE YOU all right?" were the words that greeted her as she looked into the sternly concerned face of her cousin.

"Harold, what in the world are you doing here, and why shouldn't I be all right?" she asked in total surprise. Except in passing, she had seen very little of him since breaking their engagement, and he was the last person in the world she had expected to find standing on her doorstep at this time of night.

"You took so long to answer the door, I was afraid something might be wrong. As for the purpose of my visit, I hardly think the doorstep the proper place to go into that," he said pompously, and she was surprised to realize that where at one time she had thought his ponderous attitude admirable, it now struck her as slightly ridiculous.

Not knowing what else to do, she stood aside to let

him through the door. As he walked in, his eyes went over her with critical thoroughness, his mouth tightening at her disarray. "I must say, you've been letting yourself go lately, Katherine," he said pointedly. "Perhaps you'd care to neaten up before we have our talk." Katherine found herself frantically suppressing the urge to giggle. She wondered what had ever convinced her she could marry him and live happily ever after. His Hollywood good looks and blond, sun-streaked hair were attractive enough but seemed totally inconsequential compared with Brad's dark vitality.

As though her thoughts of him were his cue for intervening, Brad stepped out of the shadows. "As far as I know, it's no crime to let your hair down when you're about to go to bed."

"What?" Harold exclaimed as he spun around, seeing the other man for the first time. Obviously trying to overcome the disadvantage of his surprise, he drew himself up to the full extent of his height, which was rather pitiful compared with the man he was trying to impress. "Who the hell are you?" he said with all the hauteur he could muster.

"I was just about to ask the same thing," Brad hinted darkly as he reached for Katherine, his arm encircling her shoulders in a possessive embrace. "Aren't you going to introduce us, darling?" he asked from between clenched teeth.

Katherine had been too confused at first to get her bearings. She had not fully recovered from the passionate intensity of the lovemaking she and Brad had been indulging in before answering the door, and she had not immediately seen the potential for misunderstanding.

"Oh, I'm sorry. I thought you knew each other," she explained helplessly.

"I'm afraid I haven't had the pleasure." Brad spoke dryly, leaving no doubt as to how much pleasure he expected to derive from the introduction.

"Oh, well," Katherine exclaimed in embarrassed confusion, "this is my cousin, Harold Hastings. I'm sure you've heard him mentioned, but I guess he came to the company after you had gone overseas." Turning to her cousin, she said, "Harold, this is Brad Donovan, Uncle Robert's son."

"And her fiancé," Brad added forcefully, then acknowledged the introduction with a marked lack of enthusiasm as his arm tightened almost painfully around Katherine's shoulders. "How do you do." Then, not even giving the other man the opportunity to answer his greeting, he continued. "And now I'm sure you'll understand if we ask you to leave. It's late and we were just getting ready for bed when the doorbell rang."

It would have been difficult to have said who looked the most shocked, Harold or Katherine. The news of their engagement was obviously not sitting well with Harold.

But he recovered quickly. Seeming wisely to judge that Katherine was the less dangerous adversary, he turned on her. "Katherine, I demand to know what's going on here."

All at once, Katherine had had enough. Embarrassment and confusion were swept aside by a very healthy anger. "Just what right do you have to come here and demand anything?" she said, lashing out at him. "Just who the hell do you think you are anyway?"

Harold's face registered the distaste he was apparently feeling at such a volatile display of emotion. "Please, lower your voice and stop swearing," he admonished her. "It's really too bad that you grew up lacking in feminine guidance. A mother's influence would have overcome your tendency to use the language of a long-shoreman."

"There's nothing wrong with her language, you mealy-mouthed little twit," Brad asserted forcefully, causing Katherine's mouth to drop open as he defended what he had always been so quick to deplore.

"My business is with Katherine," Harold retorted with more bravado than wisdom.

"Anything that concerns Katherine concerns me."

Feeling that it was time to put an end to a situation that had the potential for turning ugly, Katherine pushed her way in front of Brad. "I can handle this," she said assertively.

Two big hands settled on her shoulders and she was gently but firmly moved aside. "I'm sure you can, sug-arlump!" Brad smiled with exaggerated sweetness. "But there's no need for you to bother your pretty little head with such a small disturbance, not now that you have a man to take care of it for you."

"Just what are you insinuating?" Harold demanded with offended dignity.

"Take it any way you like," Brad replied, his smile more intimidating than a scowl would be on most men.

Whether Harold would have stood his ground was not to be known, because Katherine stepped into the fray like an avenging angel, her hair flying wildly around her, the color high in her cheeks, her eyes snapping with angry indignation. "That's it!" she exclaimed heatedly. "I've had it with you two bozos. Out, both of you. This is not Gold's Gym, it's my home, and I won't have you two idiots in it squaring off to prove your machismo. Now, get out of here!"

Both men looked stunned, as though they had suddenly been ravaged by a kitten. Harold was first to speak. "Really, Katherine, you're overreacting. I assure you that Mr., er, Donovan and I have no intention of instigating a brawl in the middle of your living room, but you must admit that you owe me an explanation."

"Speak for yourself, Hastings," Brad said curtly.

But Katherine ignored him and spoke for herself. "I owe you nothing! Neither of you, and I've had it for one night. Now, get out of here, both of you!"

She walked to the door and threw it open, standing rigidly beside it, waiting expectantly for their departure. To her relief they both appeared ready to comply with her demand as they proceeded toward the open door, Harold in the lead. As he came abreast of Katherine he looked at her meaningfully. "I'll leave now, but this isn't the end of the matter. We've got to get this business of your father's will straightened out, once and for all. You know what he wanted for both you and the company, and despite what I have discovered here tonight, I am still willing to go through with my part."

Katherine's mouth dropped open in amazement. "Oh, you are, are you?" she railed furiously when she had regained the use of her voice. "How magnanimous of you. And just what makes you think I'd have you? After what I walked in on at your apartment?"

Harold looked almost bored. "I hardly think you're in any position to point fingers, my dear," he replied as he looked disdainfully back over his shoulder at Brad. "Not after the orgy I clearly interrupted tonight. And if I'm willing to forgive and forget in order to fulfill the wishes of your father, I see no reason for your failing to do the same."

Without giving Katherine a chance for rebuttal, he

walked through the door and closed it very quietly behind him.

For a long moment Katherine could only stare at the door through which he had gone. Then she turned to Brad. "Did you hear what he said? Can you believe that? An orgy!"

It was the first time since Harold's arrival that she had taken a good look at Brad, and when she did, shock registered in her eyes, her hand flew to her mouth, and all at once she was convulsed with laughter. "Maybe Harold had a point," she gasped in between peals of laughter as she pointed her finger at him.

"What the hell's so funny," he demanded as he took her shoulders in a bone-crushing grip, giving her a shake to stop her laughter.

"We are," she told him as she tried to quell her mirth. "At least we are if I look nearly as disheveled as you do. Your hair is standing on end, there's lipstick all over your face, and . . ." She burst out laughing again, gulped, and pointed. "And my bra is hanging out of your pocket."

Brad's eyes dropped to the telltale scrap of feminine apparel. His eyes widened in shock, then his mouth twisted in amusement. "Looks like we've been found out, doesn't it?"

Katherine sobered. "Not really. I mean, we weren't really having an orgy, and you only made it worse by telling him we were about to go to bed. You didn't have to lie."

"Who was lying? And I for one feel we might as well have the game as the name. Come on, my love, you owe me an orgy."

Before Katherine knew what was happening, she found herself flung over his shoulder, her head hanging down his back, his arms wrapped around her legs.

"Put me down, you big ape!" she screamed, pounding ineffectively at his back. "What the hell do you think you're doing?"

"I told you," he stated, unperturbed at the pounding she was giving his back. "I'm about to collect on the orgy you owe me."

"I owe you nothing! Let me go!" she screamed, but found it difficult to put into the demand the authority that it deserved while hanging upside down over his shoulder.

"You've no right to do this," she added in frustrated fury as he headed for the stairs.

"Of course I do," he said with calm assurance, one arm around her knees, the other hand caressing her hip and thigh soothingly. "Every man has the right to protect his woman, at the same time making sure she knows whom she belongs to."

The slow insidious caressing of his large hand across the sensitive area of hip and thigh was making it difficult for Katherine to protest. Even hanging upside down, with the blood rushing to her head, she could feel her wayward body beginning to respond. Still, she struggled to retain her affronted dignity. "Don't talk about me as though I were some inanimate object. I'm a woman and I belong to no one other than myself."

She felt Brad's large body beneath her heave as he laughed. "You're only half right, honey," he told her, then playfully swatted her bottom. "I'll grant that you're definitely all woman, and as for whom you belong to, I think it's time you found that out, once and for all." He continued up the stairs, Katherine bobbing against his back.

As he reached the second floor he glanced around.

"Which room is yours?"

"None of your damned business!" she ranted ineffectually. "Put me down and get out of my house. I never
want to see you again!"

He shook his head. "It's too late now, sweetheart.
You should've thought of that before you asked me to
marry you. Now you have no choice. Besides, you don't
really mean it."

Didn't she? No, of course not, but by the same token
she was genuinely quite annoyed at his high-handed be-
havior. "You egotistical nerd, let me go!" she demanded,
not willing to admit the truth of what he said, but opposed
to telling an outright lie.

By this time he had located her room and marched
in, kicking the door closed behind them. "Only too happy
to oblige, my dear," he told her, a smile on his mouth.
Then without further delay he walked over to her bed
and released her, watching her bounce onto the mattress
as he began to tear off his jacket and tie.

For a moment Katherine was too astounded to realize
what he was doing, but when he sat down on the edge
of her bed and began taking off his shoes and socks, she
let out a screech of protest. "Brad Donovan, what the
hell do you think you're doing? Stop that!"

As he pulled his shirt loose from the waistband of his
pants and began unbuttoning his sleeves, she jerked into
a sitting position and began pushing at him, then tried
to redo his now unbuttoned shirt. Catching her hands in
his, Brad grinned teasingly down at her. "Be patient,
sweetheart," he murmured, deliberately misinterpreting
her actions. "There's no hurry. We've got the rest of the
night."

"We've got nothing! Now, you get dressed and get
out of here this very minute."

His eyes locked with hers; he shook his head. "Sorry, sweetheart, but I can't do that. The time has come to show you whom you really and truly belong to. There will be no more teasing and taunting me, first with my father, then with that boy you were with tonight, and finally with that worthless cousin of yours. After tonight there will be no question in your mind but that I am the man, the *only* man, in your life. So just relax and enjoy it."

With his shirt thrown aside, he turned to Katherine and put his arms around her, his weight bearing her back onto the bed. Held helplessly in his arms, Katherine for the first time in her life experienced the utter desolation of being completely subject to a man's superior strength. Her eyes wide with fearful mistrust, she looked up at him. "Don't do this, Brad. Don't force me."

"Shhh, darling," he murmured tenderly as he began to rain soft gentle kisses over her face. "I won't force you. Just relax and trust me not to hurt you. I promise I won't do anything you don't want me to."

Katherine knew then that she was lost. That had been the problem all along. She could possibly have continued fighting him, but it was impossible to fight herself. For she wanted it all, all the burning excitement she had felt with no other man.

Freeing her hands, she placed them on either side of his face and pulled his mouth to hers, putting a stop to the teasing rain of tantalizing kisses. When his mouth covered hers she made no effort to deny him the intimacy he sought, opening her mouth to grant him access to the soft, warm sweetness beyond her lips. She was drowning, time and place losing all meaning as sensation after sensation of pure ecstasy rippled through her. It wasn't until she felt his lips on her shoulder that she realized that he had dispensed with the top of her dress, but the only feeling she experienced was gratefulness as his slightly rough hands smoothed and caressed her bare skin.

Feverishly her hands explored his bare shoulders and muscular back. She was in awe of the strength and masculine aura he projected as her fingers burrowed into the thick black mat that covered his chest. Her fingernails blazed an abrasive trail through the heavy, distinctly male growth, across his chest and down the narrowing arrow ending at his belt buckle. At his moan of gratified pleasure she shivered with excitement, running her hands around his waist, then up his back.

The last barrier between their upper bodies now dispensed with, Katherine moaned with deep primeval pleasure as he pressed her bareness against him. She reveled at the feel of the stimulating roughness of his hair-covered chest against the smooth silkiness of her skin, the hardened peaks of her breasts buried in the thick mat.

A shiver of delight ran up her spine, and she moved beneath him in a circular motion, increasing the stimulation of her bare, swollen breasts against the arousing roughness of his chest.

"Oh, sweetheart," he moaned. "You drive me wild." And his mouth fastened once more on hers, hot and demanding. She opened to him completely, parting her lips, allowing him any privilege he cared to take.

Katherine had lost all sense of reality. Never before in her life had she reached such heights of excitement. Never before had she felt this desperate need to be part of another person, this absolute necessity of sharing the ultimate.

But suddenly Brad rolled over, taking her with him, wrenching his mouth from hers to bury his face in the

curve of her shoulder. His arms still held her tightly
against him until, panting with desire, she lay on her
side facing him.

Momentarily at a loss, Katherine could only wonder
at his actions. She had no fear that he had suddenly lost
interest, that he no longer wanted her, not with the evidence of his desire branding her soft belly, even through
the remaining layers of their clothing.

"Brad," she whispered breathlessly, "what's wrong?"

She felt the rumble of his laughter through every nerve
ending in her body. "Nothing's wrong, sweetheart," he
assured her, his large hand caressing the back of her
head, pulling it comfortingly to his shoulder. "Or I guess
you could say that what's wrong is that it's all so very
right. If we don't slow down, I'll explode."

Reassured, Katherine cupped the side of his face with
her hand, her long fingers gently caressing his lean cheek,
tracing the outline of his firm masculine lips, softly
brushing his thick mustache. "Would that be so terrible?"
she asked huskily. She again moved against him, squirming back and forth, rubbing her soft body against the
hardness of his. "What if I want you to explode?" she
teased seductively, marveling at this newfound wanton-
ness within herself.

"Then you're going about it the right way." Brad
groaned. "But I want it to last forever. I want to learn
every delicious inch of you, make love to you until we're
both out of our minds with it."

Katherine could only wonder at the intensity of his
feelings, for there was no doubt but that he was sincere.
He wanted her as urgently as she wanted him, but he
wanted to make it something special, something they
would both always remember with pleasure. Feeling both

exhilarated and humble, she looked deeply into his eyes and said simply, "Show me."

"My pleasure, pretty lady," he murmured, lowering his head as he once more rolled her onto her back. Once again his mouth found hers, but this time he had himself under control. Where before he had dominated, demanded, now he took time to tease and taste, to caressingly take and give exquisite pleasure.

From her lips his kisses blazed a trail downward, tasting, learning every inch of her on the way. As his tongue found the frantically pounding pulse at the base of her throat, she arched her neck, joyfully throwing her head backward, a smile of painful pleasure transforming her face.

As his lips skied the slopes of her full breasts, his large hand cupped the fullness of first one and then the other. "So beautiful," he groaned. "So very beautiful, like the finest silk crowned with the softest velvet."

His mustache brushed against her softness, bringing pulsating life to each sensitive nerve ending. And when his mouth hungrily closed over the ripeness of one of the crowning pinnacles, she went rigid, unknowingly burying her fingernails into his shoulders as she moaned, pulling him ever closer.

Reluctantly releasing its treasure, his open mouth slid down one soft white slope into the scented valley between her breasts, lingered momentarily, then ascended the twin to the prize he had so recently relinquished. "I'm a firm believer in equal opportunity," he murmured as his mouth became intensely engrossed in an occupation that prevented speech of any kind.

Moaning, Katherine twisted and turned beneath him, burning with a fire the like of which she had never before imagined. "Brad, darling," she implored. "Please," she begged, unaware of what she asked, only knowing she wanted, desperately needed, the ultimate release that only he could give her.

But he was by no means ready to submit to her pleading. With a last lingering salute to each of her swollen, pulsating breasts, he moved downward, his hands clearing away the obstruction of her clothing.

His lips paid tribute to her soft femininity, nibbling the satin softness covering her abdomen, his tongue delving the shallow well of her navel.

As his skillful hands and mouth continued to torture her tantalizingly, her own hands found the buckle of his belt. Her fingers shaking so badly she could scarcely make them obey her own command, his belt was undone, his slacks unfastened. Barely pausing in his assault on her feverish, demanding body, he raised himself up and shed the last remaining barrier between them.

Coming back down, he slid over her fully and an increased excitement raged within Katherine at feeling for the first time the bare weight of his masculinity against her. Her breath caught in her throat at the size and power of him, her flesh seeming to scorch at each contact between their bodies. She opened herself up to him fully and sighed with expectant pleasure as he lowered himself between her thighs. But still he withheld the fulfillment she craved, raising himself up, teasingly brushing her body with his.

Katherine had reached the end of her patience. "No!" she exclaimed angrily, thrusting herself forward in an attempt to forge the intimate bond he denied her, to once and for all alleviate the burning need within her.

Had she been more in control of her emotions, she might have tortured herself with embarrassment at her uninhibited lack of restraint. Instead, she only sighed with relieved satisfaction as he laughed softly before giving her that which she sought.

CHAPTER NINE

OVER MANY YEARS of being programmed to awaken at a specific time, it was very unusual for Katherine not to wake then, whether the alarm went off or not. This day was no exception. She glanced sleepily at the clock, remembered that it was Saturday, smiled lazily, and went to roll over and continue the lovely dream that had been interrupted. But as she started to move, she found herself trapped by a heavy weight lying across her waist.

Her eyes widening, she looked over to see the dark, sleeping head lying next to her on the pillow, and re-membrances of the night just past flooded her mind. It hadn't been a dream at all. It was all true. Brad had spent the night with her, and made love to her again and again, and was now lying peacefully vulnerable at her side.

She watched him in fascination, loving the way his dark lashes fanned his cheeks, the rough dark stubble of his beard, even the way his slightly parted mouth emitted soft snores. The sheet was pulled down to his waist, and she was again amazed by the strength and size of the man. She longed to once again run her fingers across his chest, feel the heat and powerful vitality that was so much a part of him, but she wasn't sure she dared. She didn't want to wake him; she was enjoying herself too much just staring at him without his being aware of it. She took pleasure in learning all the secret intricacies of his face and body, the ruffled disarray of his thick black hair, the riotous curling of the hair on his body as she reveled in the possessive way his arm held her, as though she were something precious that he didn't want to risk losing.

Smiling to herself, she nestled closer, relaxing in the warmth and security of his embrace. Within minutes she was once again asleep, a smile of happiness and contentment gently curving her lips.

It was sometime later that she again awoke. There was something annoying her, a soft tickling across her skin. Without opening her eyes she swatted at it, only to come fully awake as her hand was captured and Brad's mustache brushed against the palm as he planted a kiss in its center.

Seeing that she was awake, he smiled contentedly down into her sleep-glazed eyes. "Good morning, sweetheart," he murmured softly. His deep-blue eyes took a slow and exacting inventory of the picture she made, her honey-blond hair spread across the pillow, her lips still slightly swollen from passionate kisses of the night before, her big brown eyes warm and knowing, the soft whiteness of the slope of her breasts above the sheet.

Disconcerted by the intensity of his perusal, Katherine tried to cover her embarrassment. "See anything you've never seen before?" she said lightly.

Laughing softly, he shook his head. "But that's not to say I don't want to see it again. Some people make a hobby of watching birds; I've decided to watch you instead."

"Is that so?" she demanded with mock indignation. At that moment he could do no wrong as far as she was concerned, but she had to at least go through the motions of putting him in his place.

"You better believe it, sweetheart. Whatever you're selling, I'm buying. At this point it's definitely a seller's market."

Katherine laughed as she lifted her hand to run sensitive fingertips over the harshness of his unshaven face. "Hmmm, that's an interesting bit of information. If I'm not mistaken, that means prices are on the rise."

"I'll show you what's on the rise," he growled gruffly as he grabbed her and pulled her beneath him, his face hovering above hers for no more than a moment before his mouth fastened on hers. At first his kiss was almost brutally possessive as though to punish her impertinence, but even as her lips were parting, accepting his domination, the embrace changed tempo and became softly, seductively, entreating, tempting and tantalizing rather than threatening and punishing.

"Hmmm," he murmured as his lips left hers to slide along her cheek to the side of her face, his tongue darting into her ear, his teeth nibbling its lobe. "You taste so good this morning."

Katherine squirmed and giggled in a fashion entirely foreign to her. "Don't do that; it tickles," she said.

"What does?" he asked without remorse, continuing with what he was doing.

"Whatever it is you're doing. And what do you mean I taste good this morning? Does that mean I tasted bad last night?"

He had moved his field of operations to the sensitive skin behind her ear, and as he chuckled she could feel the vibration of his breath. "No," he assured her. "It just means you haven't gone stale overnight. Still as delicious as ever. And believe me, you were delicious."

"Were?" she asked pertly. A shiver of delight ran the length of her spine as his hand came up to cup her breast.

"Were and are," he said huskily. "The most delicious little morsel ever devised to tempt the appetite of man."

Katherine had never thought of herself as being overly feminine, the type of woman to be so tempting to men, but held so securely in Brad's arms, feeling his masculine need pressed against her, she could almost believe it was so.

"I've never thought of myself that way," she admitted while her hands, with a will of their own, measured and tested the strength of his muscular arms.

"In what way?" Brad asked, barely distracted as his lips moved lower, nibbling at the bare roundness of her shoulder before going still lower.

"You know," she said as his wayward lips kissed the white slopes of her breasts, his large hand pushing the sheet downward. "Tempting, sexy."

She gasped, her breath catching in her throat, her fingers gripping his arms as his mouth closed over the distended peak of her breast. The gentle pulling motion of his mouth sent her into a frenzy as she threw back her head and groaned with pure pleasure.

At her response Brad raised his head to look deeply into her eyes, his hands cradling her face between them.

"Take it from one who knows, sweetheart, you're sexy as all hell."

Katherine smiled up at him, staring unabashedly, imprinting his features on the screen of her mind for all time. "What makes you think hell is sexy?" she asked with a grin.

Returning her smile, he slowly shook his head. "There never was such a woman for wanting the last word," he scolded her playfully. "I thought you had learned last night who your master was, but it looks like you need another lesson."

"Oh, yes," she whispered softly through full, parted lips as her arms went up to encircle his neck. "I definitely think another lesson is called for. You've said yourself that it sometimes takes a while for me to get things straightened out in my mind."

"So I did." He smiled as she settled comfortably back on the bed, pulling him after her.

"So, professor," she teased as she kissed the strong line of his jaw, "what's the lesson plan for today?"

"The plan," he said with feigned sternness as his knee edged its way between her legs, "is to repeat the lesson of last night over and over again until you have it memorized."

Without protest she accommodated her body to his, gasping with pleasure as he settled on top of her. "Hmmm." She sighed. "I like the way you think, professor."

Laughing down at her, he kissed the tip of her nose. "So, at last it all comes out. It was my mind you were after all along."

Moving seductively beneath him, she sensually ran her hands the length of his spine, her fingers clutching the firmness of his buttocks. "How clever of you to have made such a telling discovery." She laughed up at him. Her sensitive fingertips traced erotic patterns up and down his bare back. "I just love the strength"—she paused to kiss him, pulling back a scant inch—"the size"—she punctuated what she was saying with another kiss—"the warmth of your mind." She kissed him hard on the lips. "The depth of your, um, understanding."

She teased him no longer. Once more he took control and she surrendered to him gladly, relishing his strength and domination, giving herself up to the pure sensual pleasure of being possessed by this one man, the man who would very shortly be her husband.

Having once more climbed the mountain of passion and ecstasy, they floated back gently to earth, content to lie peacefully in each other's arms. As their breathing became normal and their hearts slowed, they drifted along on a cloud of contentment, somewhere between sleep and wakefulness.

Just as Katherine was about to give in to the temptation, to let the heavy lids of her eyes rest once more, to succumb to sleep, a large hand swatted her bare bottom. "No, you don't, sweetheart," a determined masculine voice warned her. "My appetite has reasserted itself. What are you going to do about it?"

"Brad!" she retorted as she rubbed the offended area of her anatomy. "You can't possibly want to already."

Grinning at her, he quirked a thick brow questioningly. "Want to what?" he asked innocently.

After the intimacy they had so recently shared, she would have thought it impossible for him to embarrass her, but at his insistence that she put a label on the experience, she could feel the color blooming in her cheeks. "You know very good and well what!" she exclaimed. "And you can forget it."

"Denying me already," he said, moaning sorrowfully, shaking his head with regret. Then he laughed and gave her another swat. "But that wasn't the appetite I was talking about just now. Of course, if you cared to encourage me . . ."

"You need all the encouragement of a fox in a henhouse," she told him heatedly, put out with herself for not realizing it was food he was referring to. "And if you want me to feed you, you're going to have to get out of here so I can get up and get dressed."

"Why? I won't peek if you want to get up."

She looked at him skeptically, but as the need to make use of the bathroom was becoming urgent, she felt she had little choice but to trust him. Besides, it was rather silly to be embarrassed when there was no part of her he hadn't already seen. "All right," she relented. "I'll get up, but you promise not to peek?"

"You have my word as a gentleman," he assured her grandly as he lay back, his hands behind his head.

She sat for a long moment looking at him spread out across her bed, his chest bare, his strong arms lifted. He looked so good lying there, so masculine, that she was tempted to cuddle back down beside him and give him the encouragement he had previously mentioned.

"Don't you trust me?" he asked, breaking into her wayward thoughts.

"I don't seem to have much choice in the matter, do I?" she asked as she edged toward the side of the bed.

"Not much," he agreed, smiling.

"All right, close your eyes."

When they were closed she slipped off the bed and hurried to the closet, going through the clothes hanging there to find something to wear, wondering what she would be doing and whether she should put on slacks or a dress. Her thoughts were interrupted as she heard Brad say appreciatively, "You've got the cutest little bottom ever created. Actually the total package isn't half bad."

Whirling around, she glared at him, pulling at a robe that had somehow become caught on its hanger. "You said you wouldn't peek!" she protested.

"I'm not," he told her self-righteously. "I'm looking. If I were peeking, I'd have my eyes only half open. But my eyes are wide open, tickled pink at what they're seeing. Besides, how could you expect me not to look? I told you, watching you is my new hobby."

"Oh, you," she exclaimed in exasperation as she gathered up the clothes she would need. "You're completely and utterly hopeless."

"But you love me anyway," he called to her departing back.

She closed the bathroom door behind her, leaning back against it. Did she love him? It very much looked as though she did.

She took her time bathing and dressing. When she emerged from the bathroom it was to find the bedroom empty, and she looked with disgust at the tangled mess that was her bed. Quickly she striped it, remaking it with fresh sheets. Putting the soiled bedding into the hamper, she washed her hands, again checked her appearance in the mirror, and went downstairs.

Before she was halfway down she could hear Brad singing off-key and smelled the aroma of bacon frying on the stove. She pushed open the kitchen door to stand watching him. He had evidently used one of the other bathrooms, because his hair was still wet and his face was newly shaved. He was still wearing his rumpled clothing of the previous day, but he had no choice in the matter. A dish towel tied around his waist, he flipped the bacon and turned to the refrigerator, bending over to find the eggs.

Leaning against the doorjamb, arms crossed over her chest, she regarded him thoughtfully. "Now, that's what I call a great pair of buns."

Brad jumped at the sound of her voice, bumping his head on the top freezer compartment. "Damn it, don't sneak up on a man like that. You made me bump my head."

"I wasn't sneaking. *I'm* quite forthright about what I do. I don't peek, either."

Rubbing his head, he scowled at her. "You should have been spanked more often as a child. Didn't anyone ever tell you that no one likes a smartass, particularly first thing in the morning?"

"Oh, did him bump his little head?" Katherine said in mock sympathy as she went to him, pushing his hand away so that she could rub the bump for him. "Bend down here and let Mama kiss it all better. That's a brave little man."

He bent his head, but as she went up on her tiptoes to kiss his head, he intercepted her, closing his mouth over hers in a hard, dominating kiss. Katherine's arms were already around his neck as she had sought to pull his head lower, and, well-satisfied with the change in game plans, she pressed herself closer to him, burying her fingers in the thickness of hair at the back of his head.

The kiss was prolonged and just as intense as if they had not spent the better part of the past twelve hours making love to each other. But suddenly he was pushing her away, swearing as he turned toward the stove. He grabbed a hot pad. "Dammit," he muttered. "The bacon's burning, and I'm starved."

"Well, I guess that puts me in my place, doesn't it?" Katherine said calmly as she nudged him aside to take control of the situation. Scraping the charred remains into the trash, she wiped out the skillet and went to the refrigerator.

"What do you mean?" Brad asked as he leaned back against the counter, watching as she efficiently began to put together their breakfast. "What puts you in your place?"

"The fact that food is more important to you than I am. You dropped me so fast, you would have thought I was burning instead of the bacon."

Brad crossed his arms over his chest, grinning roguishly. He shook his head. "Don't you believe it, sweetheart. If you'd been the one burning, I'd have been forced to take you right back up those stairs and put out the fire."

Feeling the heat growing in her cheeks, Katherine turned to the stove. "How very magnanimous of you. You're a regular Boy Scout."

He lifted a brow and cocked his head to one side. "Hardly a boy. I thought you knew that by now. Still, we did agree that you needed your lessons repeated. After breakfast I'll be glad to go over them with you again."

"Never mind." She scowled at him as she began turning the bacon with a fork. "And if I didn't already know, you just proved all over again where your priorities lie." She nodded to the toaster. "Do you think you can make the toast without burning it?"

"If I weren't starved half to death, I'd show you priorities," he told her as he lazily unwound his length from against the counter and went to man the toaster. "But as it is, I need to keep my strength up for when we continue with your lessons."

"School's out for today," she retorted. "Now, do you want one egg or two, and how do you want them cooked?"

"Three and over easy," he told her as he put more bread in the toaster.

"Three? And do you really want all that toast, or are you just playing around now that you've finally found something you know how to do?"

"Three. I plan to eat it all. I have an enormous appetite, which I would have thought you knew by now."

Katherine ignored his pointed remarks as she broke the eggs into the skillet. While they were cooking, she set the table and poured the coffee.

As they ate there was little conversation, for Katherine found that she, too, had a hearty appetite.

After she had refilled their coffee cups, she turned to him. "Shall we take our coffee outside?"

"That sounds good. Now that I'm full and contented, stretching out in the sun sounds very appealing. Maybe I'm part cat."

Once they were on the patio he removed his shirt and lay back on one of the chaise longues, closing his eyes. Katherine sat watching him, thinking that in comparing himself to a cat, he was quite accurate. Stretched out as he was, bare from the waist up, he looked like a large contented cat, not the domesticated kind, but a large sleek jungle cat.

Just as she was beginning to think he had fallen asleep, he said, "So tell me about yourself."

"What?" she exclaimed, thinking she must have missed out on something.

"Tell me about yourself," he repeated.

"I would have thought there was very little left about

me that you don't know," she replied dryly as she sipped her coffee.

He lazily opened one eye to look at her. "I know a lot about you, but not all. For instance, I know you've got skin as soft as silk, but I don't know what your favorite color is. I know you've got heavy gold-streaked hair and a cute little rounded bottom, but I don't know what kind of music you like. I know your lips taste like honey, but I don't know what books you read. I know you've got full, beautiful breasts that swell excitingly at my touch, but I don't know whatever in the world attracted you to that wimp of a cousin of yours."

"All right, all right," Katherine protested, embarrassed at his forthright speech. "Green is my favorite color. I like most kinds of music with the exception of some of the harder rock; my preference is for easy listening. I read some of the best-sellers but really prefer a good whodunit."

She had purposely ignored his last question, but he wasn't in the mood to let her get away with it. "And your cousin?"

Katherine shrugged her shoulders and stared pensively into space. "It's hard to explain. I suppose partly I was influenced by my father. He very much wanted the match, and I guess I wanted to please him. I've always felt that I somehow let him down by not being a boy."

"That was hardly something you had any control over," Brad said dryly. "Besides, speaking for myself, I think it would have been criminal if you had been one bit different than you are."

Katherine couldn't help but be pleased by his words. "Thanks, I appreciate the vote of confidence. Nevertheless, my father made it more than clear that I was a disappointment to him. He pointed out quite often that if I married Harold, his grandchildren would still be named Hastings."

"So you let yourself be guided entirely by your father?"

She shook her head. "I wouldn't be honest if I said that. I didn't have a lot of time for dating and boyfriends while I was growing up. Father insisted that I take a double degree at the university: business and engineering. That left hardly any time for anything else. Then, too, I was the height I am now by the time I was in seventh grade, and believe me, there are very few twelve- and thirteen-year-olds, boys or girls, who are five feet ten. I felt like an oddity, a freak, and kids being what they are, my cohorts weren't shy about teasing me. By the time my peers grew up, I was too much a loner to try to make friends.

"Anyway, what with an inferiority complex big enough to choke a horse, and the demands of my studies, I hadn't had much to do with the opposite sex until I met Harold. He was good-looking and nonthreatening and I was flattered when he began to pay attention to me."

"What do you mean nonthreatening?"

Again she shrugged. "He didn't try to dominate me, either in a business sense or personally. Neither of us was overly interested in a sexual relationship." She laughed wryly. "I thought we were both blessed with a low sex drive. But that was before I found him playing house with his secretary. I think I was more shocked than hurt."

"That was also before you reencountered me," Brad suggested with a smile.

Katherine returned that smile. "It wouldn't do me much good to deny it, would it?"

He shook his head. "Not one bit." Then he returned

to the subject under discussion. "So that was what the attraction amounted to, your father's approval of him, and the fact that he didn't make you feel threatened?"

Katherine considered the question for a moment. "Mostly, but not entirely. You might have noticed the other night that he's rather stiff and formal?"

"You mean stiff-assed and pompous?"

Katherine laughed. "I guess so. Anyway, I thought for a time that that was admirable. He was all business and that's what I thought I wanted, too. But the other night I'm afraid I thought it all rather silly."

"It was silly. He's silly. He's more than silly, he's a bloody damned fool for letting you slip through his fingers. But I'm very glad that he did."

Katherine lay back on her lounge, smiling. She was very glad, too.

The afternoon and evening that followed were among the most wonderful of Katherine's life, even though she and Brad did nothing spectacular. They lay around by the pool, talking, getting to know each other, eating when they felt like it, savoring each other's company.

Once dinner was over, they retired to the living room, where Brad turned on the stereo and took Katherine in his arms. They glided across the floor, making love to the music until Brad finally picked her up in his arms and carried her upstairs to her bedroom.

They made love long into the night, Brad teasing her about her supposition that she had a low sex drive.

Sleepily she smiled at him. "I guess I just needed the right teacher, professor." With that she cuddled down beside him and was instantly asleep.

The sun was just beginning to come up over the mountains to the east when the harsh ringing of the telephone intruded into Katherine's beautiful dream world.

"Damn," she heard Brad mutter next to her, tightening his arm around her.

"I guess I'd better answer it." Katherine yawned sleepily. "At this hour it must be important." Sighing regretfully, she rolled away from Brad, wrapping the sheet around her as she went.

Picking up the receiver, she said, "Hello. Oh, Uncle Robert, good morning." She was silent, listening, the color rising in her cheeks. "What? Oh, yes, he's here. Just a minute."

She sat up and handed the receiver across to Brad. "It's your father. He wants to talk to you; he says it's important."

As she sat considering what had just happened, Katherine barely heard what Brad was saying to his father. She couldn't help but be sensitive to the fact that Robert must know they had just spent the night together, actually the last two nights. She considered herself a liberated woman, but this was still not a situation she could deal with lightly. Robert had said that it was important that he contact Brad, that Brad wasn't at home, and that he was calling her on the chance that she might know where he was.

There had been no way she could deny that she knew exactly where he was, and it was not that she was ashamed of what had happened between them during the long warmly passionate hours they had spent in each other's arms. How could she possibly regret something that had been so wonderful, so right? It was just that she would rather that it could have been kept strictly between the two of them. What they had found together was too precious to be intruded upon, too precious to be the object of idle speculation by a third party.

Brad was handing the receiver back to her. She absently hung it up, looking questioningly at him. He lay back, sighing heavily. "Trouble?" she asked.

He nodded. "The manager of our branch in Tokyo has been rushed to the hospital with a heart attack. He's expected to recover, but not for some time, if he ever gets to the point he can go back to work. Which means that I'm going to have to fly over there."

Katherine felt a terrible sinking in the pit of her stomach. "Oh, no," she cried. "Couldn't someone else do it? Don't you have an assistant manager already on the spot who could take over for him, at least for the time being?"

Brad turned to her, smiling tenderly, his long brown fingers gently circling her cheek, sliding down the vulnerable length of her neck. Leaning forward, he kissed her bare shoulder caressingly. "I don't like this any better than you do, darling, and I wouldn't go if there were any way out of it. While we do have an assistant manager, he's fairly new to the job and we're right in the middle of sensitive negotiations with the Japanese government. So I really have no choice. Surely you can understand that. Being in business yourself, you know how these things are."

"That doesn't make me like it any better." She pouted. "Damn, why did this have to happen now?" Then she frowned at her own selfishness. "That makes me sound awful. I'm sure your manager and his family are asking the same thing. I'm sorry for acting so badly."

"You couldn't behave badly if you tried." He smiled tolerantly as he leaned forward and gently kissed her lips, left vulnerable from the raw passion they had earlier shared.

Katherine laughed at his charitable attitude. "I'll remember you said that. In the past I've gotten a totally different idea about your opinion of me."

"That was before I was sure of you. Now that I know you belong to me, I'm prepared to indulge you endlessly."

"Oh, how I wish I had a recording of that to play back to you the next time you blow your top over something I've done," she hooted irreverently.

"It'll never happen," he assured her blithely as he nuzzled her neck. "And stop laughing while I'm trying to make love to you, sweetheart."

Katherine ran her fingers through his thick hair caressingly, pulling his head down to rest on her breast. "Are you trying to make love to me?" she asked huskily.

"Don't I wish." He sighed deeply. "Unfortunately duty calls." Planting a hard kiss on her mouth, he rolled away and off the bed all in one smooth motion. "If I stay in that bed one minute more, they'll have to pry me out of it." Completely unabashed by his nakedness, he walked across the floor and began gathering up his clothes.

Glancing up, he met Katherine's eyes as she sat up in bed, openly watching him. He grinned wryly. "Like what you see, sweetheart?"

"Very much. I've decided to give up bird-watching altogether. Do you mind?"

"Not at all, but you're making it awfully hard on me not to crawl back in there with you."

"I wouldn't mind."

"Don't tempt me, love. I really do have to go. Dad's made reservations on a flight that leaves in two hours, and I still have to pack a bag and stop by the office to pick up some files."

After putting on his shirt and pants he sat down on the side of the bed to put on his shoes and socks. Katherine watched with interest, loving his feet as much as the rest of him. "Can you take time to have me fix you something to eat before you go?" she asked hopefully, wanting to postpone his departure for as long as possible.

But he was shaking his head. "'Fraid not, honey. I'll grab something quick on the way." He bent forward and pulled her into his arms. "I really do hate to leave you, Katie love, and I promise you I'll be back as soon as humanly possible. Certainly before the deadline in your father's will."

"Oh!" Katherine exclaimed. "I'd forgotten all about that."

Brad laughed, his eyes gleaming. "That's the nicest thing you've ever said to me."

"That I'd forgotten my father's will? How's that?"

"You're a smart lady—figure it out for yourself." He tightened his hold on her and pressed a hard, demanding kiss on her willing lips. "I've got to go. Miss me," he ordered as he picked up his jacket and walked out the door.

CHAPTER TEN

BRAD WASN'T YET out of the door before Katherine was missing him. It was like losing a part of herself to let him go, but of course neither of them had any real choice in the matter. An event such as this was hardly unusual. There were bound to be separations now and in the future as their respective careers pulled them apart. She only wished that they could have had a little longer together, a little longer to savor the love they shared, more time for each to learn the thoughts and dreams of the other. But that would come later. They had a lifetime ahead of them, and Katherine was looking forward to the future as never before in her life.

Time hung heavily on her hands. She did the ordinary chores she always saved for the weekend, slept more than usual due to the fact that she had gotten little sleep the past two nights, and dreamed of Brad and the wonder of what they had shared. It still seemed almost too good to be true, like a fantastic dream, and she had to pinch herself to make sure she was wide awake and not fantasizing. For the first time in her life she was deeply and irrevocably in love. Anything that had gone on before was nothing compared to the love she and Brad shared. It was true that he hadn't said the words, but for that matter she wasn't sure she had said them either. There are times when actions speak louder than words, she told herself, and there was no doubt in her mind that what they shared was love at its finest.

Sunday afternoon she spent at poolside soaking up the sun. Both her body and mind were at peace. She missed Brad terribly, but she knew their separation was only temporary. Soon he would return and they would be married, and the times when they must be apart would be kept to a minimum. Yes, the future looked very rosy, Katherine thought to herself as she lay back on the lounge chair, her eyes closed and a smile on her lips.

She must have fallen asleep, because she was unaware that anyone else was near until she felt a tug on her bare toe. Sleepily she opened her eyes and saw the dark silhouette of a man leaning over her. "Brad!" she exclaimed in delighted wonder, then blinked her eyes and saw that she was mistaken. It wasn't Brad, but his father.

"Sorry, pet," Robert told her as he bent forward and kissed her cheek before taking a chair close by. "It's just your old uncle come to see how you're doing."

"Just fine," she assured him as she sat up, a bit embarrassed at seeing him for the first time since he had roused Brad from her bed. "Can I get you anything to drink?"

Seeming to sense that she needed a moment to compose herself, Robert said, "Yeah, something cold does sound good. What do you have?"

Katherine shrugged. "Probably anything you want."

"How about some iced tea?"

"Won't be a minute," Katherine assured him as she got up and slipped into her cover-up. "Do you want it out here or would you rather come inside?"

"Out here's fine. No point in living in California if you don't take full advantage of the sunshine."

Katherine smiled at him before turning toward the house. Inside, she took her time preparing the tea tray, wanting a few moments to compose herself. She was not ashamed of what she had shared with Brad, it was just so new to her. And the thought that Brad's father must know all about it was somehow disconcerting. Still, they were adults and these were liberated times. Besides, she and Brad would be married soon, and Katherine was determined not to let any thoughts of guilt or embarrassment put a pall on the opening of the most wonderful chapter of her life.

Having worked her consternation out in her own mind, she was able to smile quite genuinely as she carried the tray back out to the patio. She even chided herself for feeling self-conscious. There was no reason to worry. This was her uncle, Brad's father, and he loved them both and wanted only the best for them. Their getting together had been his idea in the first place.

Remembering that, she handed him his glass of tea and laughed as she sat down. "I guess you're feeling pretty smug, aren't you?"

Robert lifted a steel-gray brow. "Oh?" he asked innocently. "How do you figure that?"

"Don't play games with me, you old pirate. You know very well I'm talking about Brad and me. You must be dying to say I told you so."

Robert chuckled softly. "Well, now that you mention it, I *did* tell you so."

Nodding, Katherine smiled at him. "Now that you've got that out of your system, I for one don't mind admitting that you were absolutely right. At this point it feels like marriages are indeed made in heaven, not in the boardroom. I must say, though, that you're not exactly my idea of what Cupid should look like."

"Oh, I don't know. After all, looks aren't everything. Doing a good job is what counts, and I think I did an excellent job."

Katherine grimaced. "I can see quite clearly where your son got his king-size ego. He comes by it naturally."

"I can't deny that, but from the way he sounded this morning, I'd say offhand that you had something to do with the nurturing of that very same ego. So don't go blaming it all on me."

Katherine couldn't prevent a blush of embarrassment—and pleasure—at his words. It thrilled her to know that she was responsible for Brad's happiness.

"It's all right, honey," Robert told her as he reached over and patted her hand. "I shouldn't tease you, particularly when I couldn't be happier. I've known all along that the two of you would be perfect together. It was just a matter of finding the right circumstances and a time when neither of you was involved with someone else. All I had to do was pull the right strings. It wasn't hard to bring you two together."

"Yes, well, I won't complain because I can't argue with the results. But you must admit that it was a bit underhanded of you to let Brad believe that you were interested in marrying me yourself. He was livid."

Robert laughed. "I knew he would be. I loved his

expression when I told him that he could count on your having the good sense not to mother him."

Remembering the scene that had taken place in this very spot, Katherine could now see its humorous aspect, and she shared in her uncle's laughter. "It doesn't seem possible that it was only a week ago. So much has happened in so short a time."

"Sometimes things work out that way," Robert told her. "After Brad's mother died, I thought I would never be interested in another woman. And I wasn't—for years. But the minute I saw your aunt Chloe I knew my days were numbered."

Katherine lay back, absently listening to her uncle's reminiscence. When she had spoken of all that had happened in the past week, she knew Robert was thinking of her engagement to Brad. But there was more to it than that. Considering what Paul Hart had revealed last Friday, there was a very good chance that she would be confronted Monday morning with some very distressing news.

She was tempted to confide in her uncle as she had been in the habit of doing in the past, but somehow she couldn't. She felt she at least owed Harold the courtesy of verifying her facts before making public accusations. She was fairly certain of what the coming audit would show. There was, of course, the slight chance that Paul had been wrong. But she frankly couldn't see how, and she dreaded having their suspicions confirmed. She knew now that what she had felt for Harold had not been love, but the facts that he had played an important part in her life at one time, they shared a few distant ancestors, and her father had built such hopes around him. But it hurt to learn of his perfidy.

"So, have you decided when and where the wedding

will be?" Robert's voice interrupted her melancholy thoughts.

"What? Oh, no, we didn't get around to discussing it," she admitted, then blushed at the amused gleam in her uncle's eye.

"I see," he said diplomatically, not asking why they hadn't found the time to discuss such an important event, particularly in view of the deadline they were working against. "Then it might be a good idea if you make some tentative plans yourself. Brad will be home just as soon as he gets the situation in Tokyo under control, but there is the target date to consider. Have you given it any thought at all?"

Katherine shook her head. "Not really. I know it must sound foolish when it's what I was working so hard to achieve, but now that it's happening, it seems so sudden. I really never thought beyond gaining Brad's acceptance."

"You'll want to be married in church?"

Katherine nodded. "Before I didn't think so, when I thought it might be just a temporary measure, but now I want very much for it to be in church. Nothing big, I don't think either of us would be happy with some big extravaganza even if there were time to arrange it, but definitely in the church."

"That should be no problem then, as long as you want to keep it small. Would you like to hold the reception at my place?"

"That sounds like a lot of trouble for you. Besides, whom would we invite to it? Neither of us has much family."

Robert was shaking his head. "It won't be any trouble at all. I'll just call in the caterers and leave them to it. As for who should be invited, it's true that there won't be a lot of family, but you both have lots of friends and business associates who should be asked. Even so, it will still be relatively small. There's not enough time for anything else."

"Thank goodness for that. I don't think I could survive anything too elaborate."

"So, what do you say? Shall we plan on two weeks from yesterday? I know that's cutting it pretty close in terms of the deadline, but it's still within the limits, and it gives us a little longer to get it all organized. And it will give you a chance to get things at the office straightened out, to allow you time for a honeymoon."

"A honeymoon," Katherine mused, a dreamy smile on her face. "That's something else we haven't discussed. Do you think Brad will want to take one? I mean, will he have the time?"

Standing up, Robert laughed. "Of course he'll want a honeymoon. As for having the time, he'll make time, and I suggest you do the same unless you want an irate bridegroom on your hands."

· Nodding absently, Katherine continued to ponder the situation. "I wonder where we should go?"

"That I leave entirely to the two of you." Robert laughed, turning to go. "I don't do honeymoons, at least other than my own." He winked at her from over his shoulder as he walked out the gate, leaving Katherine happily considering the possibilities of different honeymoon sites.

She was still smiling the next morning as she entered the Hastings building even though she knew that the immediate future might get pretty grim, and that she would have some hard decisions to make. But nothing could diminish the pleasure she felt at the prospect of what two short weeks would bring: the beginning of the rest of her life!

"Good morning, Elizabeth," she said breezily as she headed for her office.

"Good morning, and apparently it really *is* a good morning." Elizabeth grinned cheekily. "What happened? Did you win the Irish sweepstakes?"

"Even better," Katherine said over her shoulder, laughing as she went into her office and closed the door. The time would come soon enough that she would have to share her secret with the rest of the world, but just for a little while she wanted to keep it to herself, taking it out to savor when things got difficult and she found it hard to cope. It was almost as though she were afraid of sharing her happiness for fear something would happen to jinx it.

During the week that followed, Katherine felt she was riding an emotional roller coaster. The high points were the calls from Brad, the ongoing plans for their wedding, of which he approved and which he agreed to leave in the hands of his father. The negative side of his calls was that they made her miss him even more, something that she didn't think was possible. Her only consolation was that it was obvious he was suffering from their separation as much as she was.

But the true lows of the week came in the wake of the audit company's findings regarding the company books. The discrepancy was very real and it was large. There was no way it could have been an oversight. It was deliberate and damning, and while the investigation was continuing, there could be little doubt where it would ultimately lead. In his position, Harold would have surely caught the problem had anyone else been the perpetrator, leaving only one conclusion to be drawn.

Harold had tried to contact Katherine several times during the week, but she had refused to see him, using first one excuse and then another. She was no good at dissembling and she was not yet ready to confront him. She had to wait until all the evidence was in.

She consoled her conscience by telling herself that in an attempt to be as fair as possible it was important not to jump off the deep end until she had all of her facts. Then, too, she realized that when the final results were in she would have to discuss the situation with Brad. She had offered him forty percent of an up-and-coming company, one with thriving business prospects, and it was becoming apparent that she had unwittingly misrepresented the situation. While she was sure it wouldn't affect their forthcoming marriage, she couldn't let Brad go into it under a misapprehension. Not that there was any danger that Hastings was about to collapse, but a great deal of money had disappeared, and it would take time to recoup their losses.

That, of course, was merely on the business side of the issue. While Brad had still not told her that he loved her—even though they had talked several times during the week—Katherine had no doubt that he did. What they had shared was too beautiful to result from anything other than a deep and abiding emotional commitment, one to the other. She could hardly wait for his return.

CHAPTER ELEVEN

THE FOLLOWING SUNDAY evening Katherine showered and prepared for bed, then went downstairs to watch television, hoping to be able to relax enough that she could sleep later. She hadn't been sleeping at all well over the past week. She missed Brad, and she was worried about what she should do about Harold's embezzlement of company funds. It was such a mess and she would have given anything for the whole messy situation never to have occurred. Still, she couldn't just shrug it off and take no action. Even if she talked to Harold and he promised to repay the money, he could no longer be trusted. At the very least he would have to be removed from his position. At the worst, she supposed, charges would have to be filed against him and he could wind up in jail. Just thinking about that possibility made her physically ill.

Even though she was sure it was not how a liberated

woman should feel, she was grateful that the decision of how to handle the situation was no longer hers alone. Brad was soon to become the forty-percent owner of the company, and he would definitely have a say in the final dispensation of the matter.

But when thinking of Brad she didn't like to cloud the issue with business problems. Their wedding was less than a week away. It hardly seemed possible, due in part to the fact that Brad was still away and hadn't called since the middle of the week. Sometimes it seemed almost as though she had dreamed the entire episode that had taken place between them a little more than a week ago, that she would wake up and find that the past few weeks had all been part of that dream.

When the doorbell rang, her heart leaped into her throat. It had to be Brad. When she had talked to his father earlier in the day he had said that the problems in Tokyo were under control and that Brad would be home any day. She wished Brad had called her and told her himself, but for some reason he hadn't and it was enough to know that he was here at last.

So certain was she about who it was outside, and so eager was she to see him, that she didn't hesitate for a moment to open the door, fumbling with the chain in her impatience to see the man she loved, to be in his arms once more.

"Darling!" she exclaimed as she threw the door open, her face wreathed in a smile of welcome that fell miserably when she saw her mistake.

"For a minute there I thought you had finally come to your senses." Harold scowled as he entered, pulling the door out of her hands and closing it behind him. "But it wasn't me you were expecting, was it? It was Donovan."

Not waiting for an answer, hardly looking at her, he

crossed the hall, went down the two steps into her living room and directly to the bar. He had been in her home often enough that he was no stranger to it, and he unerringly found the Scotch and poured a generous amount into a glass, taking a deep, steadying swallow.

"What are you doing here, Harold?" Katherine asked wearily. She had no desire for a confrontation at this point. When the time came she wanted to have all of her facts at hand, and even then she wanted the interview to take place in front of at least one witness. Besides, her disappointment that it hadn't been Brad at her door was overwhelming, and all she wanted was the privacy to cry her frustrations out in peace.

Harold's mouth was twisted in a mocking sneer. "It wasn't so long ago that you wouldn't have dreamed of asking me a question like that," he said acidly. "You were always only too happy for me to drop by."

Katherine felt the heat of anger racing through her veins. Any sympathy she had been feeling for him fled as she listened to his taunting remarks. She didn't know why he was here, but her temper was spiraling higher and higher with each minute he stayed. "There's no point in discussing what may or may not have been. It's all in the past. This is the here and now and you're no longer a part of my life and no longer welcome to just drop in whenever you feel like it. Now, I'd like you to leave."

Taking another swallow of his drink, Harold glared at her from over the rim of his glass. "I'll leave when I damn well please," he growled. "I'm sick to death of taking orders from you, watching you throw your weight around. You and your sanctimonious father, always the people in charge while poor-relation Harold is supposed to be grateful for every crumb that falls from your table."

Momentarily shocked out of her anger, Katherine said,

"I didn't realize you felt that way, Harold."

His mouth twisted derisively. "And you never took the trouble to find out, did you? As long as you kept 'Daddy' happy, that was enough for you."

Katherine couldn't help feeling a certain guilt, because there was more than a grain of truth in what he said. She hadn't seriously considered Harold's feelings during their relationship. He had merely been the means to an end. But if that were true in her case, the reverse was also true.

"Perhaps there's some truth in what you say, but then, you were using me, too. You never really cared anything about me personally, you were only concerned about what you could get from me."

"Don't be vulgar, darling." He grimaced, and Katherine could not suppress amusement over the fact that he was still trying to maintain a stiff dignity, regardless of the circumstances.

"As for getting anything out of you," he continued, "to date, I've gotten very little, but that's about to change."

"What do you mean?" Katherine asked with uncertain wariness.

"I mean, my dear cousin, that one way or another I plan to get control of Hastings. I've got it coming after all the years I've spent licking your old man's boots. And just for the record, I know what you've been up to, getting those auditors in behind my back."

"Then I suppose you know what they found?"

He nodded offhandedly. "But it hardly matters. The money is mine, or soon will be."

"I don't know how you figure that. You only own twenty percent of the company."

"For the present. But make no mistake, Katherine, I aim to get what's rightfully mine. I need that money,

and I'm going to have it no matter what it takes to get
it."

For the first time since he had entered the door
Katherine felt an icy shiver of fear run up and down her
spine. She remembered that she and Brad had laughed
at him as a figure of fun, but there was nothing funny
about the way he was acting now. He was very determined, and obsessed with getting what he considered his
rightful due. How he meant to go about it, she had no
idea.

Sinking down on the edge of the sofa, she nervously
pulled the edges of her robe closer together. "You're not
being rational, Harold," she tried to reason with him.
"Besides which, you've been drinking. Why don't you
go home now and we'll talk about it later?"

Harold threw back his head and laughed without restraint. "You'd like that, wouldn't you? A nice pat on
the head and I trot along like a good little boy. Well, it
won't work, my dear. I've been drinking, but I'm not
drunk, and I'm here to stay—at least until we get this
straightened out. Now, the way I see it, you can go ahead
and marry me as we had planned or you can promise to
let the deadline in your father's will expire without marrying anyone. After that, I don't give a damn who you
marry so long as it doesn't interfere with my taking
control of Hastings."

Katherine couldn't believe his effrontery. "But you
will be so good as to let me marry you if I choose to?"
she asked with unconcealed rancor.

He shrugged, seating himself beside her on the couch.
"If you like," he agreed with blatant disinterest.

"How magnanimous of you, but you'll excuse me if
I decline your very gracious offer."

He finished off his drink and set the glass on the coffee

table. "Suit yourself. It doesn't matter that much to me, one way or the other. I just thought I'd let you have the chance of being equal partners. This way I'll own sixty to your forty percent, but if you're satisfied, who am I to complain?"

"Your generosity overwhelms me," Katherine retorted sarcastically. "But this is all rather pointless when I marry Brad next Saturday. You'll get no more of the company than what you have right now."

Shaking his head, he said, "You're not listening, Katherine. I said you will either marry me or you'll marry no one until after the deadline has past. Now, which will it be?"

"Why don't you take a flying leap straight to hell?" Katherine asked with mocking sweetness.

Just then the doorbell rang once more, Katherine's heart began to pound because she knew who it had to be. She couldn't be mistaken. She started to get up to answer the door, but as she rose Harold put his foot in her way, tripping her. Brutally he grabbed her arm until she had fallen in a heap across him.

She struggled to right herself, but his arms closed around her in a grip of steel. "Let me go, you fool!" she said angrily. "There's someone at the door."

"Then they'll just have to wait, won't they? And don't call me a fool. I've taken all the abuse from you that I intend to."

Again she tried to twist free, but she was only hurting herself. She heard the front door open just as Harold roughly covered her mouth with his.

"What the hell is going on here?" Brad exploded as he bounded down the steps into the living room.

Before Katherine could clear her mind of confusion or open her mouth to speak, Harold raised his head and said, "Oh, Donovan, it's you. As you can see, you're interrupting. Surely you'll excuse us, we were just on the point of going to bed." He seemed to take pleasure in using the same words Brad had used previously, under similar circumstances.

The look on Brad's face was terrible to behold, and before Katherine could open her mouth to deny it, he had grabbed her arm and forcibly wrenched her out of Harold's embrace. With his hands bruising her shoulders, he held her in front of him, shaking her as though she were a rag doll. "Is he telling the truth?" he demanded.

"No, no," Katherine protested. "He's lying. He forced me, he's arranged all this, he . . ."

"By God, woman, you'd better be telling me the truth," he retorted as he pushed her aside and grabbed the front of Harold's shirt, jerking him to his feet.

"Now, just a minute, Donovan. Take your hands off me. Can't you see she's lying? She invited me here tonight. Said she had decided we should patch up our differences, that she wanted to marry me as we had originally planned."

"You little creep. You're lying through your teeth." Brad pulled back a massive fist and caught the smaller man in the midsection, sending him sprawling, knocking over the coffee table and a plant stand as he went.

Harold lay lifelessly among the debris, but Brad grabbed at him again. As he did so, Katherine at last snapped out of her dazed stupor and ran to them. Pulling at his arm, she cried, "Brad, stop it. You'll kill him!"

Brad shrugged her off. "What of it?" he snapped.

She caught at him again. "No, Brad, don't!"

With indifferent ease he threw Harold back onto the floor and Katherine was afraid that her cousin might be dead or dying. Panic-stricken, she ran and knelt beside him, her hand feeling along the base of his throat, searching for a pulse. She felt the reassuring beat against her fingers and drew a sigh of relief. "Thank God he's all right," she whispered fervently.

"You're grateful?" Brad demanded incredulously. She looked up to see him towering threateningly above her, looking like an avenging god of old with his hair flying every which way and his eyes snapping with wild resentment. "If you're telling me the truth, that scum was trying to compromise you," he said harshly. "Or maybe he was right. Maybe you'd rather I left so you could get on with it."

The hour just past had been the most traumatic of Katherine's life. She had actually been assaulted, the shock of it all searing her very soul, but the implication of what Brad was saying gave rise to her very healthy temper. Jumping to her feet, she faced him, her hands on her hips, her eyes flashing.

"Maybe you should go straight to hell, too, Brad Donovan! How dare you say something like that to me? Of course I'm grateful that you didn't kill him, not because it would be any loss to me personally, but because I was stupid enough to worry about what would happen to you if you'd killed him. Murder is against the law, you know. They put murderers in jail for a long time— if they don't execute them. Naturally I didn't want that to happen to you, though why I should care, I don't know, when at the moment I'd like nothing better than to kill you myself. You big ape, I missed you, I needed you, and then you come in here acting like—acting like . . ." All at once the anger drained out of her and the realization of what had so nearly happened descended on her in a weight that was too heavy for her to carry.

She collapsed onto the edge of the divan, her elbows on her knees, her face in her hands.

For a long moment Brad was speechless as he stared down at her, then tentatively he put a hand on her shoulder, softly whispering her name.

Looking up, Katherine stared at him through grief-stricken eyes, the tears running heedlessly down her cheeks quietly, soundlessly testifying to her unbearable distress and sorrow, wordlessly condemning him for his callousness.

"God!" He groaned wretchedly as he dropped down beside her and pulled her into his arms. "I'm sorry, sweetheart," he whispered as he feverishly smoothed her hair away from her wet face, his lips tasting, drying the tears from her cheeks. "You know I didn't mean it. Forgive me."

Her face still felt bloodless, but with her eyes brightly brimming with the love she felt for him, Katherine looked up and smiled tentatively as though still unsure of his reaction. "Darling," he moaned, and holding her face firmly between his hands, he lowered his mouth to hers.

And in her extreme relief Katherine responded whole-heartedly, all doubts and fears forgotten in the heat of his passion and her own need for comfort and reassurance. Deeply, eloquently he tasted her, hungrily kissing her again and again, his hands sliding over her body, bringing her warmly to life after the cold and fear of the trauma she had so recently experienced.

At the sound of a loud banging they drew apart, their eyes questioning each other across the few inches that separated them. Some degree of sanity returning, Katherine glanced sideways to where she had last seen

Harold lying insensibly across the floor. He was no longer there. "It must have been Harold leaving," she suggested hesitantly.

"Good riddance," said Brad as he reached for her again.

But she twisted her head aside. "Shouldn't we stop him? He's been drinking quite a lot, and now he'll be driving."

"I imagine he's sobered up considerably over the past five or ten minutes," Brad said prosaically. No longer trying to hold her captive, he looked around at the chaos he had helped to create. "This place is a mess," he said as he stood up. "Why don't you get me a large trash bag and I'll help you clean it up."

To have him offering to help her clean house was something of a comedown after the heat of the passion they had shared moments before, and if Harold had sobered up, he didn't have a thing on Katherine. As she went through to the kitchen, she tried to analyze the situation, make some sense out of what had taken place. She was still too shocked to be able to look at it objectively. The main focus seemed to be the fact that Brad had saved her from Harold's cruel, unexpected, and unwanted attentions. It still seemed something of a miracle when she remembered how hopeless had been her position, how ineffectual her struggles as she had tried to free herself. If Brad hadn't shown up when he did . . . She shuddered just thinking about it.

After the room had been put to rights they sat beside each other on the divan, sipping hot coffee, and incredibly, in view of what they had shared in the past and the experience of that evening, the silence between them was strained as though each was afraid of initiating a conversation for fear of disturbing the status quo.

"How did your trip go?" Katherine said at last, then felt stupid because that was not at all what she had wanted to say. Still, it broke the silence and that was something.

He looked at her over the rim of his cup. "Fine," he said. "The contract is signed and the assistant manager is proving very capable. He should be able to handle things."

Again a silence descended. This time it was Brad who broke it, and his comment was at least a bit nearer to their more intimate concerns. "Dad tells me everything's taken care of as far as the wedding plans go."

Did she detect a hint of dissatisfaction in his voice? "Yes. It's scheduled for next Saturday. Does that present a problem for you?" Dear God, she thought to herself, they sounded as though they were discussing an upcoming board meeting. What was wrong? Had he changed his mind?

"No, no problem."

Again silence fell between them, a crackling, electricity-charged silence, and at last Katherine had had enough. Sitting up, she faced him. Throwing her hair back over her shoulder, she thrust her chin out aggressively. "Look, Brad, if you've changed your mind, just say so."

"Changed my mind? About what?"

"About the wedding, you idiot! If you don't want to marry me, just say so. You're not the only man in the world." Even as she was saying it, she knew it wasn't true, at least not as far as she was concerned. He *was* the only man in the world for her, and it was pure nerves that made her imply differently.

Brad slowly rose to his feet. "Such as that boy I caught you with last week?" he asked grimly. "I thought I had made it clear that you were to stay away from him. Have you been seeing him again?"

"Of course I've seen him," Katherine stated defiantly. "After all, he does . . . Brad!" she squealed as he grabbed her up into his arms. "Put me down! What do you think you're doing?"

"I thought you had learned last week just what the score was, but it appears you need another lesson," he said grimly as he headed for the stairs.

Katherine's first inclination was to resist his high-handedness, but even as she opened her mouth to protest, it occurred to her that she was being ridiculous. This was what she wanted, what she had dreamed of for a solid week. Why fight it?

Calming, she relaxed in Brad's arms as he carried her up the stairs and into her room, her face nuzzling the curve of his throat.

He walked to the bed and dropped her, then stood staring down at her, his hands on his hips. "Why is it I get the feeling I've been had?" he asked, an indulgent smile twisting his lips.

"I can't imagine what you're talking about," she replied innocently. "As far as I know you haven't been had—yet. But I live in hope."

"Oh, you do, do you?" Brad smiled as he slowly began to undress, seeing the pleasure reflected on Katherine's face as she watched him. "If this is too much for you, you could always turn your head, you know."

"And miss the show? Not on your life. If the bottom ever falls out of the electronic component field, you could make your fortune as a male stripper. You're beautiful. Just add a little music, effective lighting, and you've got it made."

"You, my beautiful little torment, are asking for it," he threatened as he lowered himself beside her.

Lifting her fingers, she brushed them lightly across

the corner of his mustache to gently caress the line of his jaw, the dimples on the sides of his mouth. Her eyes glowing, she looked lovingly up at him. "I knew you'd get the idea sooner or later."

"Minx," he growled as he leaned over her, bearing her back into the softness of the mattress. He stared down into her dancing eyes, only inches from his. "You deserve everything you're going to get," he said playfully.

"Promises, promises." She laughed, staring up into his face.

His mouth swallowed the laughter from her lips as his mouth captured hers in a forceful kiss. "I'll show you promises," he muttered as his mouth left hers briefly to explore her face, her neck, her shoulders. "One of us is definitely wearing too many clothes," he grumbled as he tried to forge his way to the soft temptation of her swelling breasts.

"You're a smart man; why don't you come up with a solution?" she said even as he was already taking care of the matter in his own way.

Within seconds she was lying naked in his arms, and she sighed and cuddled closer. "I knew you'd think of something," she murmured happily.

"I'm nothing if not inventive," he agreed as he pulled her onto her side facing him, his hand running the length of her spine, pulling her closer and causing a shiver of delight to pulse through her body.

"And I just love a man with an inventive mind," she told him, her fingers molding the planes of his face, raking through his thick hair.

He gave her a stinging slap on her bare bottom. "Just *one* man with an inventive mind," he told her. "I can see you're going to need further training before you've learned your lesson."

Had she planned to complain at his rough handling,

she wasn't given the chance as his mouth closed over hers, his body following her over as he pushed her flat on her back. By the time he had released her mouth she had forgotten to be angry with him. And when his hungry mouth found her throbbing breasts, she surrendered completely to him and to the glorious explosion of the sensual delight he had initiated.

Raising his head from hers, he stared down at her, his eyes burning a trail from the top of her head to her feet, then reversing. "I thought I must have been fantasizing, that my memory of you couldn't possibly be a reality, but you're even more beautiful than I thought. You are totally and completely beautiful."

"Oh, Brad!" She pulled his head down to hers, opening her mouth, and thrust her tongue forward to do erotic battle with his.

When Brad at last wrenched their lips apart, they were both breathing heavily. He buried his face in her throat. She moved against him, wanting to get closer, but he stilled her. "No, sweetheart, slow down. I'm so hungry for you, I could go up in flames, but I want to make it last, to reacquaint my lips with every delicious inch of you."

His actions followed his words as he rained kisses over her face, down the side of her throat, pausing to taste the beat of her heart pulsing at its base.

By the time his mouth reached her breasts she was groaning with agonized pleasure, her head thrown back, her fingers digging into his shoulders. His lips closed first over one extended peak, then over the other, his tongue circling, tantalizing, causing her to cry out his name in supplication.

"God, how I've missed you," Brad groaned as his lips continued their downward journey. "I didn't know it was possible to want someone as much as I've been wanting you."

"Me, too," Katherine moaned incoherently. He was driving her crazy with wanting him, with the burning need deep inside her.

He was just kissing the bend of her knee when she became aggressive. Heaving herself upward, she pushed him over onto his back.

"What?" he asked as he looked up at her hovering over him.

"Turnabout is fair play," she said, laughing down at him. "If you can drive me crazy with your teasing and tantalizing, then I should be able to return the favor."

He lay back and relaxed, a smile lighting his face. "I'm very much in favor of equal rights. Help yourself."

And she did. Her mouth tasted his beautifully molded lips, the strength of his throat, his muscular shoulders. She buried her face in the thick curling hair on his chest, following the descending arrow down his flat hard stomach.

At last he could take no more. "Enough," he gasped as he gathered her beneath him and united their bodies in a hot, wild, uninhibited dance as old as time.

Once again Katherine woke to find herself sharing her bed with a man. Not just any man, but as Brad had prophesied, *the* man, the only man she ever wanted to share her life with. Lazily she let her gaze wander over him as he slept. Even in his unkempt condition, hair rumpled, face unshaven, she thought he was beautiful and she smiled, remembering his reaction when she had told him so the night before.

Impulsively she used the index finger of her right hand to gently brush across his mustache, then moved down-

ward to caress his sensuous lips. She stroked them in
one direction and was just beginning the return trip when
his mouth flew open and he bit down on the tip of her
finger.

"Ouch, you cannibal!" she said as she jerked her finger
free.

"That'll teach you to start without me," he admonished, smiling.

"I don't know what you're talking about," she replied
with innocence.

"Not much, you don't," he said as he grabbed her and
smothered her mouth with his.

When he finally came up for air she was rosy and
breathless and noticed that he was watching her intently.
"You're even more beautiful than you were last night,"
he murmured huskily.

"So are you," she replied dreamily, all pretense of
indignation gone.

He playfully swatted her bottom. "I am not beautiful,"
he said firmly.

"Ouch, stop that," she ordered as she rubbed the offended part of her anatomy. "And if that's the way you're
going to act, then I agree, you're not the least bit beautiful!"

Chuckling, he displaced her hand with his own to rub
and smooth her imagined injury. "Now you've got it. I
am not beautiful . . . Handsome, yes; sexy, definitely; but
beautiful, no."

"Big-headed, absolutely; egotistical, without a doubt;
a big bully, guaranteed!" she squealed as he grabbed for
her. "Brad, stop it!"

"I can't," he growled. "I'm a big-headed, egotistical
bully who's about to have his way with you."

"Not now you aren't. Brad, stop it! Look, Brad, look

at the time! I have to be at work in forty-five minutes."

"So you'll be late for once," he replied unfeelingly. "What's the good of being boss if you can't be late once in a while?"

Katherine felt her resolve weakening as his hands and mouth made shambles of her puny defenses. "But it's important that I be there today. It's something I need to talk to you about," she protested, then moaned her surrender as he pulled her beneath him.

"We'll talk later," he assured her as all desire for conversation drained out of her.

Katherine was an hour late when she walked through the door of her private suite of offices.

"Oh, there you are." Elizabeth looked up, smiling as Katherine came in. "I was getting worried about you and just finished calling your house to see if you were all right." She cocked her head inquiringly. "Some guy with a deep sexy voice said you were on the way?"

She made it a question rather than a statement, but Katherine was in no mood to satisfy Elizabeth's curiosity, even as she realized she was compounding the problem as she tried valiantly, but not very successfully, to suppress the telltale color rising in her cheeks. She had left Brad fixing himself a substantial breakfast after refusing to take the time to share it with him. She didn't blame Elizabeth for her interest, and she would have to explain Brad's place in her life soon, but not now.

"I'm meeting with the auditors in fifteen minutes. Let's get as much of the mail taken care of as we can before they arrive," she said as she walked through to her office.

The morning was a busy one and proved every bit as dismal as Katherine had feared it would. The audit had shown beyond a shadow of a doubt that Harold had embezzled a sizable sum of money from the firm. Upon inquiry, she found that he had not come in to work that morning. She called his home but received no answer. She was in a quandary as to what she should do next. She shied away from the prospect of initiating criminal proceedings, but she supposed it would eventually come to that.

She had wanted to discuss the matter with Brad that morning but had been sidetracked, very pleasantly side-tracked, she remembered. A few weeks ago, she had had no idea she could be the sensuously giving and taking lover she had become in Brad's arms. Until then she had thought that such stories of "passion on a grand scale" were little more than fairy tales. She had always seen herself as a level-headed businesswoman and had had little time for discovering that she was first and foremost a woman. Whatever the future held, she would be satisfied to be allowed to share it with Brad.

Her one remaining doubt regarding their relationship was the fact that he still had not told her that he loved her. He had made such beautiful love to her over and over again, making her feel cherished and adored, but he had never once said the words that she longed to hear. Surely after they were married he would be able to say them. Just five more days until their wedding. It seemed a lifetime.

The day was long and busy. After learning for certain the exact amount of the deficit caused by Harold's foray through the Hastings computer system, she had begun the complicated process of deciding ways and means of minimizing the damage to the overall operation of the firm. If worse came to worst, she might have to divert some of her personal funds to cover part of the loss. It was not something she would do ordinarily, but this case was anything but the norm.

She had been hard at it all day, not even leaving her office for lunch. Instead, she absently chewed on a dry sandwich as she continued to fuss and fume over the problems dumped in her lap as a result of Harold's duplicity. When her intercom buzzed at five-thirty she stretched, easing the tension in her back, then answered the summons.

"Is it all right if I bring in your letters for signing now?" Elizabeth wanted to know.

"Of course. I'm sorry, I forgot the time. You should have reminded me sooner," Katherine said apologetically.

"No problem," Elizabeth assured her as she switched off the intercom and almost immediately came through the door, closing it behind her. She laid the letters on the center of Katherine's desk and waited with suppressed excitement for her to finish signing them.

As Katherine affixed her signature to the last one she looked up and noted Elizabeth's bright-eyed excitement. "What's going on? You look as though you just broke the jackpot."

"More likely it was you who did that."

A frown creasing her forehead, Katherine rubbed her temples to ease the headache that had been threatening all day. "I'm really not in the mood for games, Elizabeth. What are you talking about?"

She had not meant to be curt, and was glad that her remark appeared not to be taken that way.

"Rough day, huh?" Elizabeth sympathized. "Well, there's something in the outer office that should make it all better. The package containing that sexy voice I told you about this morning just walked in and wants to see you. Talk about truth in advertising! He's even better than expected."

"Brad's here?" Katherine said as she rose from her chair, a hand automatically rising to smooth her hair.

Elizabeth nodded, watching her employer's reaction with unfeigned interest. "Shall I send him in?"

Before Katherine had time to ask for a few minutes in which to freshen up, the door opened and Brad stuck his handsome head around it. "No need." He smiled as he walked into the room. "I'm already in."

He walked around Katherine's desk and pulled her into his arms, completely oblivious of their interested spectator. "Hello, darling," he murmured softly as he looked down into her eyes. "Miss me?"

"Brad! Not now!" she admonished him, thinking of the eyeful Elizabeth must be getting, then drew a sigh of relief as she heard the door close behind her discreetly retreating secretary.

Sighing, she rested her head on his broad shoulder. "Now you've done it," she scolded him halfheartedly.

"What have I done?" he asked as he tipped her face up and gently kissed her closed eyes.

Katherine felt her pulse accelerate. "Blackened my reputation in the eyes of my secretary."

"Don't you believe it," he told her as his lips nibbled a path across her face and down her neck. "She looked to me as though she would have liked to cheer me on."

"She probably would," Katherine admitted. "She thinks my social life is a terminal case."

"Then she'll be glad to know that the miracle cure has been discovered, won't she?" Brad teased.

She pushed him away, punching at his chest. "A miracle yet! You really do think highly of yourself, don't you, Brad Donovan?"

"No higher than I deserve, soon to be Mrs. Brad Donovan."

Katherine lowered her head, feeling the heat in her cheeks, her heart beating overtime. "I like that," she said quietly.

"See, I knew you'd see the light and come to appreciate my true worth," Brad said.

"Not that, you idiot. I still think you're the most conceited, overbearing man I've ever met. I was talking about the Mrs. part. I like it," she admitted openly.

"Oh, sweetheart," he murmured. "So do I." And his mouth found hers in a long, draining kiss.

When he lifted his head from hers, they were both breathless. "We had better get out of here," he told her raggedly. "before I'm tempted to lay you down on that desk and make love to you amid the papers, pencils, and computer terminal."

"That should put an end to any shred of reputation I might have left," she told him, laughing as she turned away to gather up her purse and briefcase.

They were seated at a table in a popular seafood restaurant waiting for their meal when she brought up the subject that she had been wanting to discuss for so long. "Brad, there's something I must talk to you about."

Brad looked at her with suspicion, noting the seriousness of her expression. "Yes?" he replied warily.

Katherine frowned, aware of his less than receptive mood. This might not be the most propitious time for a discussion of a matter that could have serious repercussions, but she felt she had no choice. It was essential that some action be taken soon.

"I hardly know where to start," she admitted. "I guess

I should begin with Paul. You remember Paul Hart, don't you?

"I'm not likely to forget," he assured her curtly. "What's the matter? Have you suddenly discovered you have a taste for cradle-robbing?"

"What are you talking about?" she demanded in angry frustration, not understanding why he should be so hostile.

"You know very well what I'm talking about. Just what the hell is that boy to you, anyway?"

That battle had to be put on hold while the waiter served their food.

"That *boy*," Katherine fumed once they were again alone, "happens to be a very competent computer operator and a valued member of my accounting department. I owe him a great deal."

Brad stabbed unseeingly at the food on his plate. "When it comes time to pay him what you owe him, just make damn sure you remember you belong to me. We're getting married in five days and you'll regret it if you try getting out of it at this stage of the game."

"I have no intention of trying to get out of anything," Katherine muttered from between clenched teeth. "And I resent the implication that my relationship with Paul is anything but business. Now, will you shut up and let me explain?"

"I'm waiting," Brad replied generously, appearing to have relaxed somewhat at her assurance that it was business they were discussing.

"Thank you so much," Katherine replied. "Now, the fact of the matter is that Paul came to me over a week ago with some disturbing suspicions. He had been checking out our accounting procedures as they are programmed into the computer system, and what he found was disquieting."

"There were discrepancies?" Brad asked, suddenly alert.

Katherine nodded. "We stayed late at the office that night and he showed me exactly where his concern lay. Neither of us could come up with a logical explanation, so I called in an auditing company. They gave me their final report today."

"And?"

Katherine laid her fork on the edge of her plate, folded her hands tightly in her lap, and looked him unflinchingly in the eye. "There have been several hundred thousand dollars misappropriated from company funds."

"And the thief?"

Katherine winced at the brutal starkness of the word. Her eyes dropped. "Harold," she said so quietly that he could barely hear her.

"Hastings? He's the one who was stealing from you?" Brad sounded outraged.

"He said last night that he didn't consider it stealing, that he was just taking what was his, or soon would be."

"You mean that was his reason for being there in the first place? He wanted to beg you not to prosecute?"

"Not exactly. Oh, he knew the auditors were in, and I suppose he realized that if I didn't yet know what he had done, it was only a matter of time. That's why"— she stopped to take a deep breath—"that's why he thought that if he could force me to marry him, or at least not marry you, it wouldn't matter what he had done."

Brad's face looked thunderous. "You might have told me all of this earlier, last night or this morning."

From the time she realized Brad must eventually be

told the details of the situation, and given the opportunity to back out, Katherine had not known quite what to expect. She had never seriously thought, however, that he would actually want to take the escape route she planned to offer him. Now she was no longer sure. Suddenly she felt she was talking to a cold and distant stranger rather than to the man with whom she had shared her most intimate moments.

"I tried to tell you," she insisted defensively. "But you didn't give me a chance."

"I would have thought that such a resourceful lady as yourself could have found a way if you had really wanted to," he said accusingly.

On the point of arguing with him, Katherine brought herself up short. Perhaps there was a certain amount of truth in what he was saying. If she had really been determined she could have found a way of telling him, but she had told herself she had wanted to see the auditors' report first. Actually she had also been afraid of his reaction. Rightfully so, as it now appeared.

Her dinner long forgotten, she sighed deeply. "Look, Brad, there is nothing to be gaining by fighting between ourselves."

"You're right." He surprised her by agreeing. "The question now is what are you going to do about it?"

"You mean about Harold?"

"Yes, about Harold," he mimicked hatefully. "What have you done about the fact that he has stolen a great deal of money from you? Have you called in the authorities?"

"Not yet, I was waiting—"

"Waiting for what? For him to have a chance to get out of the country?"

"No, damn you!" Katherine exclaimed, then looked

around to make sure no one else had heard. She was discovering that a public restaurant was not the most ideal location in the world for a confrontation of this sort, but then there had been distractions at home, too. Better not to think of that, because it was beginning to look as though there would be no more pleasurable distractions of that kind in the future. She had told herself that the problem with the company would have no bearing on her personal relationship with Brad, but apparently she had misjudged him. He certainly wasn't behaving like a man who felt a few hundred thousand dollars lost for love was unimportant.

"Whether you believe me or not, I didn't want to do anything until I had discussed it with you. I felt that as you stood to become the owner of forty percent of the company, you should have some say in how something of this magnitude was handled."

"And how do you want to handle it?" he asked, not giving any indication of his own feelings.

Katherine shrugged. "I'm not really sure. If possible, I'd rather not have any adverse publicity. Not if it can be avoided, anyway."

"In other words, you want to let him off scot free."

"That's not what I said, but on the other hand I don't know that there's a whole lot of choice. It would be different, of course, if we had gone public with our stock, but as it is, there will be no one involved but the three of us."

"And you expect me to go along with letting that little bastard get away with it?"

"Keep your voice down," she warned him.

"Then let's get the hell out of here," he growled as he stood up without waiting for her agreement. Neither did he extend her the courtesy of escorting her to the door but instead, after carelessly throwing several bills on their table, turned and stomped on ahead, leaving her to make her way by herself.

Once they were in the car they were silent, seemingly by mutual consent to have suspended hostilities until they were once more in the complete privacy of her home.

As she walked in and looked around at her surroundings, Katherine could hardly believe it had been only a few short hours since she had left so optimistically that morning. Still warm from Brad's arms, she had been foolish enough to believe that there were no difficulties they couldn't overcome together. Apparently she had been wrong.

Brad went to the liquor cabinet and poured himself a stiff drink, not offering to get one for her. "So now that we can't be overheard, let's hear again about how you plan to let your cousin go without so much as a slap on the wrist," he said grimly.

"I didn't say that," she told him, her patience stretching thin. "Naturally he would no longer be allowed to work for the company, and I would hope that he could eventually pay the money back."

"My, my, aren't we being stern," Brad taunted cynically.

"Despite what you seem to think, my concern is not for Harold but for the company. We just signed an important government contract. This kind of scandal could put it in danger, not to mention jeopardizing future business possibilities."

There followed an uncomfortable silence between them. Finally Brad sighed resignedly. "I don't know why you bothered to consult me. It seems that you already have the solution worked out to your own satisfaction."

"I'm not saying that this is the only possible solution.

I am simply explaining why I think it the best way of dealing with the situation."

"If I don't agree, will you do it my way?"

Katherine shrugged. "I don't know. I have yet to hear what your way is. Do you have another solution, one that will still keep it out of the papers?"

Brad rocked back on his heels, pensively studying the amber liquid in his glass. "I'm not sure. I'll have to think about it."

"Well, here's something else for you to think about," she retorted recklessly. "One reason I wanted to explain the situation to you was to allow you to reconsider our engagement. When I proposed, I thought I was offering you forty percent of a solidly solvent enterprise. I now find that's not exactly the case. While there's no question of our going under, the shares are quite obviously not worth what they once were."

He looked at her steadily, and Katherine felt her heart fall down around her ankles. If he had truly loved her, if he had not been marrying her for the sake of the Hastings shares, surely he would have spoken up immediately to tell her so. Instead, he just stood there watching her.

Finally he put his glass down and walked toward the door. "I'll let you know," he said as he closed the door behind him.

CHAPTER TWELVE

JUST LIKE THAT he left. Katherine stood, stunned, staring at the door through which he had just exited. She could hardly believe it, it had all happened so quickly. This very morning, just a few short hours ago, she had experienced the greatest happiness she had ever imagined possible, and she had thought it had meant something to Brad, too. But apparently she had been wrong. Otherwise he surely wouldn't have calmly walked out on her.

In reply to her offer to release him from their engagement, he had said, "I'll let you know." But there was no doubt in Katherine's mind what he was really saying. It had been obvious. He was no longer interested.

The rest of the evening Katherine walked around as though she were in a trance. While she knew she was living and breathing, she felt as though the very core of her being was dead. How, she wondered, could one man have come to mean so much to her in such a short time?

She couldn't explain it; she only knew it had happened. And now he was gone and she wanted to curl up and die.

Almost as though she had switched to automatic pilot, she went through the motions of preparing for bed. She showered, dressed in her nightgown, and crawled into her lonely bed. For some time she lay staring at the ceiling, remembering the joy that had been hers in this very bed just twenty-four short hours ago. And then the tears began to fall, and as if a dam had burst, she cried with greater intensity, her entire body racked with sobs.

At some point she dropped off to sleep, but when an alien sound disturbed the quiet, she was instantly alert. She lay stiffly, the sheet gathered in her fist above her breast, her eyes open wide, her head cocked, listening.

Then it came again. There was someone in her room! She opened her mouth to let out a blood-curdling scream, but as the first sound left her throat, a large hand clamped itself across her mouth.

"What the hell are you trying to do, wake the entire neighborhood?" a gruff voice growled.

Katherine collapsed into a relieved heap at the sound of Brad's voice. Whatever else he might do, he wouldn't harm her physically.

He reached over and turned on the small bedside lamp. "I'm sorry if I scared you. I didn't mean to."

He sat on the edge of the bed watching her. "Have you been crying?" he asked.

She rubbed the back of her hand across her cheeks, dismissing the tenderness she saw in his expression. "Of course not," she blustered bravely. "I've told you, I don't cry."

His grin showed his disbelief. "Of course you don't. Silly of me to have forgotten."

Not feeling up to sparring with him, Katherine asked the question that was uppermost in her mind. "Brad, what are you doing here?"

"I came to bring you something." He got up and walked to the chair where he had hung his jacket, and she realized that must have been what had disturbed her sleep. But what was he doing in her bedroom at that time of morning? And taking his clothes off? Did he think she would tolerate a simple affair with him? Or had he decided after all that he wanted to marry her?

He soon disabused her of that notion. Taking something from the pocket of his jacket, he walked back to the bed and held it out to her. "I wanted to give you these and tell you that we no longer have to get married."

"I see," Katherine mumbled numbly, not seeing at all.

"Here, take it," he ordered as she lay silently staring up at him, her heart breaking all over again. "I sure as hell went to enough trouble to get them for you since that seems to be the one thing you really want."

"I don't understand." She barely spoke above a whisper. "What is it?"

"Papers that virtually make you the sole owner of Hastings Electronics."

"But how? I don't understand," she repeated.

"It's simple enough." He sighed as he sank tiredly down on the edge of the bed and threw the packet of papers into her lap. "It seemed to me that there was nothing so important to you as your father's company. I don't know, I'm no psychologist, but I suppose it has something to do with your relationship with your father and your feeling that you had to prove yourself worthy. Whatever it is, it doesn't matter anymore.

"As to how I got those"—he nodded toward the unopened packet—"first, I paid Cousin Harold a visit. It didn't take a lot of convincing, in view of the circumstances for him to agree to sign over any and all rights to Hastings he has now or may have in the future."

"Harold did?" she asked in amazement, then was suddenly struck by an unpleasant thought. "You didn't hurt him, did you?" she asked anxiously.

"No, I damn well didn't! At least not much," he ruefully amended. "At any rate, he was only too happy to do anything that would keep him out of prison. Anyway, after getting his signature on the dotted line I visited a lawyer I know, and then discussed the situation with my father, who, as you know, is the estate's trustee, and I am now assured that there will be no bar to your claiming full ownership."

Katherine couldn't speak. She just lay there staring at him in stunned silence.

"And so," he continued, "that's what I meant when I said we didn't have to get married. Your father's will is virtually invalid."

Katherine swallowed the lump in her throat. "It appears you've gone to a lot of trouble to get out of marrying me," she murmured huskily, the pain of it tearing her apart.

But Brad was shaking his head. "You misunderstood. I didn't say we weren't getting married. I said we no longer *have* to."

A faint ray of hope took root in Katherine's heart. "Brad, what are you saying?" she whispered.

He took her hand in his and raised it to his lips, kissing first the smooth back of it, then opening her fingers to plant a kiss in the warm palm before once more curling her fingers over it. "I'm saying, my darling Katie, now that there is nothing standing between us, nothing to force us to do something we might not want to do, will you marry me? Please?"

The hope in her heart bloomed full. In amazed wonder she read the love for her reflected in his eyes. "Brad"— she hardly dared to breathe—"do you love me?"

"From the moment you opened the door to me that first night," he admitted. "And each time I see you it gets worse, until you have me so tied in knots I hardly know which way is up."

"But you never told me," she said accusingly.

"How could I? It seemed clear that your first concern was always the company. That kind of competition is rough on a man's ego."

"There's nothing the matter with your ego," she assured him. "Besides, you surely didn't think it was the company I was concerned with when I let you make love to me."

"Well, no, that was the most fantastic experience of my life and I couldn't help coming back for more, every chance I got. But in the hard light of day I was still afraid that if you hadn't needed me to secure your inheritance, you wouldn't have wanted to tie yourself down."

Katherine lay there shaking her head in amazement. "For a smart man you're remarkably dumb," she told him candidly.

"Is that so?" he growled as he grabbed for her.

But he needn't have worried, she wasn't going anywhere. "Yes, that's so, you big bully. And if you don't stop fooling around and kiss me this minute, I'm going to beat you within an inch of your life," she threatened.

"Really, darling," he said, grinning down into her laughing brown eyes. "I didn't know you were into kinky sex, but I'm willing to try anything once—if that's what turns you on."

He lowered his mouth to hers and knew within seconds what it took to turn her on. It would be some hours before she got around to accepting his proposal.

WONDERFUL
ROMANCE
NEWS:

Do you know about the exciting SECOND
CHANCE AT LOVE/TO HAVE AND TO HOLD
newsletter? Are you on our *free* mailing list?
If reading all about your favorite authors,
getting sneak previews of their latest releases,
and being filled in on all the latest happenings
and events in the romance world sound
good to you, then you'll love our SECOND
CHANCE AT LOVE and TO HAVE AND
TO HOLD Romance News.

If you'd like to be added to our mailing list,
just fill out the coupon below and send it
in...and we'll send you your *free* newsletter
every three months — hot off the press.

☐ *Yes, I would like to receive your free*
SECOND CHANCE AT LOVE/TO HAVE
AND TO HOLD newsletter.

Name _____

Address _____

City _____ **State/Zip** _____

Please return this coupon to:

Berkley Publishing
200 Madison Avenue, New York, New York 10016
Att: Rebecca Kaufman

74

HERE'S WHAT READERS ARE SAYING ABOUT

Second Chance at Love®

"I think your books are great. I love to read them, as does my family."
— *P. C., Milford, MA**

"Your books are some of the best romances I've read."
— *M. B., Zeeland, MI**

"SECOND CHANCE AT LOVE is my favorite line of romance novels."
— *L. B., Springfield, VA**

"I think SECOND CHANCE AT LOVE books are terrific. I married my 'Second Chance' over 15 years ago. I truly believe love is lovelier the second time around!"
— *P. P., Houston, TX**

"I enjoy your books tremendously."
— *I. S., Bayonne, NJ**

"I love your books and read them all the time. Keep them coming—they're just great."
— *G. L., Brookfield, CT**

"SECOND CHANCE AT LOVE books are definitely the best!"
— *D. P., Wabash, IN**

*Name and address available upon request

Second Chance at Love®

All of the above titles are $1.95
Prices may be slightly higher in Canada.

Available at your local bookstore or return this form to:

SECOND CHANCE AT LOVE
Book Mailing Service
P.O. Box 690, Rockville Centre, NY 11571

Please send me the titles checked above. I enclose _____ 75¢ for postage
and handling if one book is ordered; 25¢ per book for two or more not to exceed
$1.75. California, Illinois, New York and Tennessee residents please add sales tax.

NAME_____

ADDRESS_____

CITY_____ STATE/ZIP_____
(allow six weeks for delivery)   **SK-41b**